"Would It Help If I Apologized For Kissing You Last Night?"

"A lady usually doesn't like to hear a man say he's sorry for kissing her," Ella replied, stepping away from the stove.

Hawk had expected her to give a sigh of relief. Instead, she faced him down with a spatula and the most refreshing sincerity he'd encountered in years.

"What do you suggest we do, then? Would silverware at ten paces be fitting?"

"I prefer steak knives myself."

"Perhaps if you'd be willing to call a truce, I'd offer to set the table." Hawk reached around her to open the silverware drawer.

The lightest touch of his arm against her body was enough to set her imagination sailing for erotic destinations. The thought of those arms wrapped around her waist... Of his big, masculine hands caressing her... Of stepping back and cuddling her body against his in a fit as perfect as the two spoons he lifted out of the silverware drawer...

Dear Reader,

Welcome to the world of Silhouette Desire, where you can indulge yourself every month with romances that can only be described as passionate, powerful and provocative!

Fabulous BJ James brings you June's MAN OF THE MONTH with *A Lady for Lincoln Cade*. In promising to take care of an ex-flame—and the widow of his estranged friend—Lincoln Cade discovers she has a child. Bestselling author Leanne Banks offers another title in her MILLION DOLLAR MEN miniseries with *The Millionaire's Secret Wish*. When a former childhood sweetheart gets amnesia, a wealthy executive sees his chance to woo her back.

Desire is thrilled to present another exciting miniseries about the scandalous Fortune family with FORTUNES OF TEXAS: THE LOST HEIRS. Anne Marie Winston launches the series with *A Most Desirable M.D.*, in which a doctor and nurse share a night of passion that leads to marriage! Dixie Browning offers a compelling story about a sophisticated businessman who falls in love with a plain, plump woman while stranded on a small island in *More to Love*. Cathleen Galitz's *Wyoming Cinderella* features a young woman whose life is transformed when she becomes nanny to the children of her brooding, rich neighbor. And Kathie DeNosky offers her hero a surprise when he discovers a one-night stand leads to pregnancy and true love in *His Baby Surprise*.

Indulge yourself with all six Desire titles—and see details inside about our exciting new contest, "Silhouette Makes You a Star."

Enjoy!

Joan Marlow Golan

Joan Marlow Golan
Senior Editor, Silhouette Desire

Please address questions and book requests to:
Silhouette Reader Service
U.S.: 3010 Walden Ave., P.O. Box 1325, Buffalo, NY 14269
Canadian: P.O. Box 609, Fort Erie, Ont. L2A 5X3

Wyoming Cinderella
CATHLEEN GALITZ

Published by Silhouette Books
America's Publisher of Contemporary Romance

To my personal fairy godmother, my agent,
Denise Marcil, who has dedicated her life
to making others' dreams come true.

 SILHOUETTE BOOKS

ISBN 0-373-76373-5

WYOMING CINDERELLA

Copyright © 2001 by Cathleen Galitz

This edition published by arrangement with Harlequin Books S.A.

® and TM are trademarks of Harlequin Books S.A., used under license.
Trademarks indicated with ® are registered in the United States Patent
and Trademark Office, the Canadian Trade Marks Office and in other
countries.

Visit Silhouette at www.eHarlequin.com

Printed in U.S.A.

Books by Cathleen Galitz

Silhouette Desire

The Cowboy Takes a Bride #1271
Wyoming Cinderella #1373

Silhouette Romance

The Cowboy Who Broke the Mold #1257
100% Pure Cowboy #1279
Wyoming Born & Bred #1378

CATHLEEN GALITZ,

a Wyoming native, teaches English to seventh to twelfth graders in a rural school that houses kindergartners and seniors in the same building. She lives in a small Wyoming town with her husband and two children. When she's not busy writing, teaching or working with her Cub Scout den, she can most often be found hiking or snowmobiling in the Wind River Mountains.

One

"**W**hat kind of a father are you?"

Bleary-eyed, Hawk looked up from his computer screen to discover what appeared to be a crazy woman standing before him. Surveying her from head to toe, he was struck first with male appreciation of her lush, young figure. Next he noticed that hair the color of flaming autumn leaves had escaped its once tight bun and was now hanging to the side like a hat askew. A tear in her nylons ran up the front of one shapely leg, disappearing beneath a faded skirt that he found too short to suit his own professional standards. On a personal basis, however, he found it quite pleasurable to consider. The angry sparks shooting out of those astonishing green eyes made him glad the stranger didn't appear to be armed.

It had never occurred to him that he might need a guard in such isolated Wyoming backcountry.

The question the woman posed resonated in Hawk's

mind like a sonic boom echoing off canyon walls. It was
the same question he'd been asking himself ever since his
wife had died, turning his life upside down and leaving
him to assume full parental obligations without a clue as
to how difficult that was going to be. It had come as quite
a shock to this well-respected corporate executive to discover that it was far harder keeping track of two head-
strong children than overseeing a company of fawning
employees tripping all over themselves to do his bidding.

And speaking of independent children, one didn't need
particularly impressive powers of deduction to figure out
who had let this intruder into his house. Flanking her on
either side, the culprits, his children—five-year-old Billy
and his four-year-old sister, Sarah—each held one of the
interloper's hands.

Not the kind of man used to having his parenting ability
questioned, Hawk didn't take well to such impolite interruptions—even on those rare days when everything was
going right. Today was not such a day. He had burned
breakfast, fought with Sarah over the necessity of combing her hair, stubbed his toe on a toy truck parked in the
middle of the kitchen and spilled orange juice on an important contract. All the while trying to juggle a multi-
million-dollar deal in cyberspace. One more power outage
like the last one and Hawk vowed to throw his state-of-
the-art computer right out the window and purchase one-
way tickets back to New York for the whole family.

"I beg your pardon," he said in a chilling voice that
he usually reserved for imbeciles and unwanted salesmen.

"As well you should," the crazy lady responded, waving a broken high heel at him. Clearly the businesslike
demeanor that set many a corporate executive trembling
in his expensive Italian shoes didn't affect her in the least.
"I have half a mind to report you to Social Services!"

"Half a mind?" Hawk mumbled in feigned confusion, making the threat sound like an indictment of the woman's mental state.

As if laboring under the impression that he suffered from a dull mind, she formed her words carefully and delivered them slowly.

"I am your neighbor, Ella McBride, and at the risk of offending you, I'll repeat myself. I want to know exactly what kind of a father lets his children wander willy-nilly about the countryside without any regard to what might happen to them. Do you have any idea how dangerous that can be? Need I mention snakes, bears and ne'er-do-wells?"

Shaking his head in confusion, Hawk turned his full attention upon his children who quickly ducked behind their unlikely protector. Dawning comprehension registered in his rugged countenance. Terror leapt in his eyes. His stomach churned at the thought of what could have happened to his children all the while he assumed they were safely tuned in to their favorite cartoon in the den.

"Do you mean to tell me that you two left this house without my permission?"

A roar would have been less frightening than that softly put question.

Ella felt a twin tremor run through the children cowering behind her.

The children felt her quiver as well.

Never in all her life had a voice affected her so. Like whiskey, it had the power to make her feel loose-limbed and giddy. Making an improvised comb of his fingers, the man ran them through a thick shock of hair the color of molasses. His sideburns were tinged with silver. Very distinguished looking, Ella decided, tucking a stray tendril of her own unruly hair behind her ear. Instantly she regretted the self-conscious gesture.

She wasn't here to gawk at this gorgeous hunk of manhood, but rather to give him a well-polished piece of her mind. Ella knew better than to accept his sudden concern and elegant surroundings at face value. Some of the nicest homes in which she'd been placed had housed the worst monsters.

How dare her hormones sabotage her self-righteous anger!

It mattered little to Ella that he didn't look at all like the villain she had envisioned on her death march over here. He had neither the broken blood vessels nor bulbous nose characteristic of a heavy drinker, nor the hooded eyes of someone who has something to hide. In fact, the man surrounded by stacks of important-looking papers was exceedingly handsome.

That all too feminine observation only served to make Ella even angrier. As far as she was concerned the question she asked was purely rhetorical. The fact that he was more interested in what was going on with his computer than with his children was answer enough.

"Just because you have money doesn't give you the right to divest yourself of your parental obligations," she snapped.

After traipsing first from her property to his and then from one exquisite room after another, searching for someone to accept responsibility for these two dirty-faced cherubs, Ella's sense of moral indignation was on full burn. Surely anyone living in such luxury should be able to afford decent child care.

"Come out from behind there, you two," Hawk said, rising from his chair. "And tell me what's going on."

It irritated him to see Billy and Sarah cowering behind

a complete stranger like she was Saint Michael the archangel sent expressly to rescue them from his fury. Hawk knew that they were giving this young woman the impression that, on top of being negligent, he was an ogre, too.

The pair stepped timidly out from behind her to face their father's anger. Ella kept a hand glued to each child's shoulder, giving them both a reassuring squeeze.

Though the concern reflected in this man's eyes made her doubt he'd ever actually laid a finger on either of them, Ella remembered being beaten for far less in the name of "discipline."

"Maybe it would be better if I talked this over with the children's mother," she suggested.

Hawk couldn't have agreed more. "I'm sure it would. Unfortunately, since their mother just recently died, I'm afraid I'll have to do."

Ella was taken aback. Despite her best effort to remain angry, her heart softened.

"I'm sorry," she offered lamely. "How long ago?"

"Not quite a year."

She was sorry for asking. Aside from it being none of her business, there was little she could do to help other than to bend down and give both children a deeply felt hug. As tears welled up in little Sarah's eyes, Ella felt moisture rise to her own. She knew firsthand what it felt like to lose a mother at such a young age.

As much as she would have liked to comfort the poor child, time was a commodity that she scarce could afford. Glancing at her watch, she wished she could somehow stop its hands from ticking onward by sheer willpower alone. Regrettably, time refused to accommodate her. Any other day, she might have welcomed an adventurous hike through the thicket to meet her rich new neighbors. Today, however, she was late for an interview. And while it may not be the most glamorous job in the world, it was one she desperately needed. The growing mountain of rejection letters piled atop her desk confirmed the dismal reality that unrecognized creativity paid even less well than slinging hash.

Ella checked her watch again.

If her truck decided to cooperate, the trip into town would take the better part of twenty minutes, leaving barely enough time to compose herself before facing the prospect of yet another dead-end waitressing job. That time frame did not allow for the return hike over a game trail connecting her property to that of the children who had shown up unannounced on her doorstep earlier that morning.

The pair had looked as bedraggled as the litter of kittens that somebody had so "kindly" dumped on her property a couple of weeks ago. Mewling in the rain, they begged to be taken in and properly cared for. Belatedly Ella realized that it had been as great a mistake to offer these young callers their fill of chocolate chip cookies and milk as it had been to feed the kitties that had promptly taken up permanent residence beside her rusty wood-burning stove. An orphan herself, Ella had a soft spot in her heart for any abandoned creature.

Telling herself that these children were not her responsibility did little to ease her conscience. When those chocolate-smeared faces looked at her as if they'd somehow stumbled upon the home of the good fairy, she could no more abandon them than she could have let any hapless stray starve to death.

"We've been living with our grandma and grandpa," Billy offered helpfully.

"Just until I could arrange to move the family out

here," Hawk interjected. He didn't want this young woman to think he was the kind of father who dumped his responsibility on his aging parents. Parents who were no longer physically up to the challenge of raising young children.

"I was hoping a geographic change would do us all good," he continued. "Unfortunately, I misjudged the difficulty of running a business via computer. Power outages are such common occurrences way out here in the boondocks that I have to admit to having second thoughts."

The look of chagrin upon that handsome face made him appear far less formidable than he had only minutes before. In fact, Ella found herself fighting the surprising urge to gather him up in her arms and comfort him as well. The provocative thought sent blood rushing to her face, making her feel all of sixteen again.

"On top of everything else," Hawk proceeded, eager to share his worries with another adult. "The lady I hired as a nanny ran off with a truck driver two days ago, leaving me completely in the lurch."

By way of explanations, Ella had to admit this one was first class. She'd come marching over here all set to turn this man into the local Social Services agency and found herself mentally retracting every rotten name she had called him on the way over. All things considered, some of them had been unusually harsh.

"I'd plugged the kids into a video an hour ago hoping I could buy enough time to complete a crucial business transaction. It never occurred to me that they would wander out of the house. I know it's no excuse," he scolded himself.

Squatting down to look his children directly in the eyes, he did something that took Ella totally by surprise. He gathered them into his arms and said, "I don't know what you two were thinking, but don't ever, ever do that again. I don't know what I'd do if anything were to happen to you."

Had she not been standing there, Ella wondered whether this macho man might have actually allowed himself a tear or two of relief. Watching him, it was hard not to wonder how differently her own life might have turned out had her own father shown half the concern that this man was displaying.

Glancing up in her direction, Hawk suddenly became very businesslike. "I'm sorry to have burdened you with my troubles, Miss McBride."

"Please call me Ella." She wanted to make certain these children knew she wasn't completely forsaking them. "As your closest neighbor, I'd be more than happy to take both of you for a walk sometime so your daddy can get caught up on his work. Just make sure you ask in advance and that he escorts you over to my place."

Checking her watch again, she came to accept how hopelessly late she was. Short of catching a flight with the next scheduled superhero, there was no way she was going to make that interview on time now.

"I'm sorry to have inconvenienced you," Hawk said, genuinely contrite. "I'm deeply indebted to you. If you haven't already gathered as much, my children mean everything to me."

Even so, Hawk hated to be beholden to anyone. If there was a way to settle the score, he would like to get it out of the way now before this young woman discovered how truly wealthy he was. Having encountered more gold diggers in his life than he could count without the aid of a calculator, he was leery of accepting favors from anyone. Long ago he had given up on the idea of anyone doing him a good turn without an ulterior motive.

"I'd be more than happy to pay you for your trouble," Hawk offered, reaching into his pants pocket for his wallet.

Ella looked startled.

Hurt.

"Certainly not," she responded stiffly. "But if you wouldn't mind me placing a long-distance call on your phone, I'd really like to try rescheduling an interview that I'm in the process of missing right now."

Again she felt the man's eyes perusing her appearance. Knowing she must look frightful after trekking through the underbrush, Ella scowled at him. After all, it was his fault that she looked so disheveled. Her sense of moral obligation had taken its toll. Beneath the heat of the day, she had wilted like a store-bought rose. Her best shoes, which had not been designed for overland excursions through tangled brush, were completely ruined. And a glance in the mirror near his desk showed red marks across her cheek, scratches that attested to branches smacking her in the face. By the time she straggled inside this luxurious home, she looked better prepared to apply for a job as a safari guide than a waitress.

She most certainly did not need this particular hunk to make her feel even less attractive than usual. Abandoned by her father at birth and orphaned by her mother's premature death ten years later, Ella was past the preferred age of adoption when she entered the state's social system. Each time a prospective parent passed her over for a baby, a toddler, or a prettier, blond, blue-eyed little girl, she became convinced that her own freckled-faced, red-haired—the bane of her existence—plain looks were not going to get her anywhere in this world. So instead she chose to cultivate other attributes like diligence, competence, loyalty and a fertile imagination that could take her far beyond any institutional walls.

The children's father didn't return Ella's scowl. Instead a dazzling smile spread across his face. One could almost see the proverbial lightbulb going on over his head.

"I've got a better idea," he said, stepping forward and pinning her with a gaze that could best be described as predatory.

Startled, Ella took a step backward and tripped over the arm of a plush chair.

Hawk reached out a hand to stop her tumble in midair.

At his touch, Ella felt a whoosh of air leave her lungs. Her lips formed a perfect "O" that filled the room with an exclamation of astonishment. A zing of electricity passed from his hand to hers, locking them in a current of pure sexual energy. Ella's pulse skittered. Her eyes widened in surprise. His, she noted, were the most remarkable shade of gray shot through with golden flecks, and they sparkled with male awareness. And if she wasn't mistaken, he was no more immune to the electricity generated by their touch than she was.

Ella wasn't sure what had gotten into her. Never in all her life had a man affected her so immediately. So entirely.

"Are you okay?" he asked, a knowing grin tugging at the corners of his mouth.

Had her knees actually turned gelatinous? Ella wondered as she attempted to steady herself. She might not be the prettiest doll on the shelf, but she'd always prided herself on being graceful. And relatively quick-witted.

This klutz act was downright embarrassing.

She hastened to assure herself as much as him. "I'm fine. Really."

Removing her hand from his was like tearing two magnets apart. It took an act of supreme willpower. Grateful that she had somehow managed to break contact with him physically, Ella deliberately stepped around the offending chair and placed it between them as a barrier.

Hawk suppressed a grin. Surely this sweet little thing didn't think he was going to chase her around the furniture like some lecherous villain in a moldy, old situation comedy. As a successful international business entrepreneur and widowed father of two, he was way past playing those kinds of silly games. Burdened by responsibilities which he shouldered himself, he hadn't entertained thoughts of a sexual nature for so long that it was actually comical. For goodness' sakes, Ella McBride was just a child herself. A virgin, too, he'd bet by the way she'd reacted to his touch. Why, the poor thing was practically hyperventilating.

"There's no need to look so frightened," he said, hoping to avoid having to instruct her on how to breathe deeply into a paper bag. "I have no intention of forcing myself on you. I just want to offer you a job."

Ella's eyes narrowed suspiciously. "What kind of job?"

"None that requires you dressing up in a sexy French maid's outfit if that's what you're worried about," he assured her with an irresistible smile that had her reaching for that chair all over again.

Digging her nails into its velvet upholstery, Ella did her best to look aloof and sophisticated. It was obvious that this man found her a funny, naive little fool. Which, of course, she was. What would anyone as obviously rich and handsome as this man want with an ugly duckling like her? Certainly not the sexual dalliance that she had imagined for the split second that had sent her pulse racing full speed down that long, well-traveled road of her imagination.

"Not only do I feel terrible about causing you to miss your interview," Hawk assured her. "I really could use your services. Clearly my children are taken with you."

Considering that it might well take a crowbar to pry them from her side, it was a gross understatement.

"And I really do need your help."

"Are you asking me to be your nanny?" Ella asked in dismay.

What was it about her that gave off such strong maternal vibes? She felt far too young to be pigeonholed so early as a full-time caregiver. Having just discovered how full life could be on her own, she wasn't overly eager to give up her freedom just yet.

Misunderstanding, Billy began jumping up and down in excitement. "Yeah, you can be our new mommy!"

Even though she didn't know exactly what was going on, Sarah, too, began dancing in place and chanting, "Mommy, mommy, mommy!"

"Nanny!" Ella and Hawk corrected in chorus.

Seeing the becoming blush coloring her cheeks pink as apple blossoms, Hawk tried smoothing over the awkwardness of the moment. "That word has such a menial connotation. Couldn't you just think of it as helping out a desperate father and children?"

Desperate was too mild a word for how Hawk was feeling. Over the past year he had developed a new appreciation of what such "menial" work entailed. Backbreaking, exasperating, and unappreciated, it nonetheless had intrinsic rewards that could never be found in a boardroom. After Lauren's death, Hawk came to realize just how much distance his job had put between him and his family. For a time he'd felt more like a stranger than a father. The children were only just now beginning to open up to him. Being included in their nighttime prayers, reading them their favorite stories and feeling their little arms wrapped around his neck in a tight hug was all the incentive he needed to work out whatever problems might arise. Working at home would give him the opportunity to forge that precious connection with his children. Having someone to help him oversee them while he attempted to run a business was the perfect solution to provide for their safety and his sanity.

Price was no object in procuring this young woman's services, and "no" was not an answer Hawk was accustomed to accepting.

Ella fended off the suggestion with a wave of her hand. "It's kind of you to offer, but I really don't think so."

"Please," little Sarah implored, her huge blue eyes filling with hope.

Ella groaned.

She recognizing the throbbing behind her right eyeball for what it was.

Obligation overload.

That all too familiar sense of having to put others' needs before her own was so deeply ingrained from years of service that it had left worry lines permanently etched upon her forehead. Passed over for adoption herself time and time again, Ella was frequently farmed out to foster homes in need of a strong back and free baby-sitting services. Her friends had called her Sister Mac in jest, making fun of her devotion to other people's children—and reminding her of the heartbreak she inevitably suffered every time those ties were severed.

Years of being used by the system had taught her the folly of putting herself second to others more fortunate.

"Pleeeeeease," echoed Billy, dragging the word and her heart into several pieces.

"Do you mind my asking what you planned on making if you got that job in town you mentioned?" Hawk asked before the final decibel of his son's pleading had died away.

The offended look on Ella's face indicated that she did indeed mind. Nonetheless she rattled off a figure that included a fair margin for gratuities. She may not be the prettiest girl George Abrams would ever hire on at the Watering Hole, but she had a way with customers that unruffled feathers and transformed frowns into smiles. People found Ella's genuine interest in them so refreshing that even the crustiest curmudgeons usually left a generous tip behind.

Hawk didn't so much as blink at the sum she quoted. "I'll double it. And include room and board as well as a generous up-front signing fee. How soon can you move in?"

"Move in?" Ella squeaked. "Why, I don't even know your name!"

"William Fawson Hawk III," he supplied in a formal tone, extending her a smile and his hand once again. "But you can just call me Hawk."

Ella backed away from it as she would from a snake curled up in the grass. She wasn't about to risk physical contact again with anyone who held such phenomenal power over her sensibilities.

"If you're a decent cook, I'll triple the amount. The kids can testify to the fact that I can even manage to screw up a basic peanut butter and jelly sandwich, and even their unnatural fondness for microwave macaroni and cheese has worn thin."

"I can cook, and I can provide you with references,

too,'' Ella admitted grudgingly, feeling herself slipping into the vortex of the tornado which was gathering speed around her. Her head was spinning. Was this guy for real?

Looking around at the sophisticated decor, Ella knew she wasn't dealing with just any crackpot. It appeared this man was an excellent businessman, just as smooth as the expensive bourbon she'd spied behind the wet bar. Did he realize that he was offering her an opportunity to make enough money over the course of a year to pay for the college education that had been eluding her since high school graduation? If she continued taking classes one at a time as she could afford them, Ella figured she'd be old enough to collect Social Security by the time she actually earned a degree.

Why she wasn't jumping all over this man's extraordinary offer was beyond her.

It certainly wasn't because she minded doing an honest day's work. She had been doing that for as long as she could remember. Nor did it have anything to do with not liking the two little imps who had wolfed down an entire sack of cookies at her rough-hewn table. They were utterly adorable. Not to mention that they could well prove to be the most valid audience to whom she could safely subject her stories. Even though a heartbreaking stint of trying to make it as a full-time writer/illustrator hadn't yielded the slightest opportunity of being published, Ella wasn't ready to part with her dream until she absolutely had to.

Perhaps it was because as an aspiring artist, she was reticent about giving up her solitude.

Perhaps it was simply that she had already wiped enough runny noses and bottoms to last her a lifetime.

Or perhaps it was because the impact of this man's eyes was as powerful as his touch. A touch, she reminded herself nervously, that sent her tumbling over a chair like some cheap slapstick comedian.

"How soon can you start? Will you need help moving in?" Hawk pressed.

The lopsided smile he had passed on to his son deepened the dimple in his chin that Ella found so fascinating. Such charm ought to be bottled, she thought, dimly aware that she was being danced into a corner without so much as feeling her feet touch the ground.

"I can help," Billy volunteered, throwing his little chest out in a manly fashion.

A woman would have to be made of marble to have resisted such chivalry.

Ella capitulated with a sigh that said she already regretted the decision. "Moving isn't a problem. I don't have much to bring over," she explained simply, then added with an authority that belied her youth, "but if I'm going to work for you, we need to establish some ground rules."

Hawk tried not to grin too broadly. He didn't think he could keep a straight face if she started setting forth conditions to safeguard her chastity.

She didn't. Instead Ella startled him with an admonition that had nothing whatsoever to do with protecting her lithe young body.

"I'll agree to your terms as long as number one, I can have every Wednesday evening off to attend a college class I've already signed up for, and number two, you agree not to undermine my authority in any way. I want free reign to handle the children how I see fit. I have to warn you," she added looking him squarely in the eye with all the earnestness of someone about to disclose a long, checkered criminal record. "My methods are less than conventional."

"With hair such an outrageous color of red as yours, I'd expect no less," Hawk proclaimed, filling the room with the warm resonance of a laugh that left Ella's face flushed.

Two

The next day, as she snapped her suitcase shut, Ella was still fuming about Hawk's parting remark. Scratched and scuffed from years of abuse, the old yellow luggage had indeed seen better days. But as it was one of the few things Ella had left to remind her of her mother, it was nonetheless an item she cherished. Setting the solitary bag out on the porch, Ella thought to herself that it was a good thing being a nanny didn't require an extensive wardrobe. A couple of pairs of jeans, a few T-shirts, her favorite red sweater, and a pair of tennis shoes would have to serve her well.

As had the rustic cabin which she had called home for the past year and a half. The single room was large enough to house a bed, a rough-hewn table, a couple of chairs and an ancient but functional stove utilized both for cooking and heating purposes. An easel stood guard beside the front window. Colorful art supplies were neatly arranged in a box beside an unfinished work in progress. Log walls were decorated with vibrant paintings of castles and fairyland inhabitants, several wearing the latest in modern-day running shoes.

Others might turn up their royal noses at the thought of living as simply as Ella did, without such newfangled conveniences as running water and electricity. Disregarding their judgment as bourgeois, she laughingly referred to her home as a "studio." Ella considered herself in good company with other artists who accepted hardship as a necessary encumbrance in maintaining the freedom of their unconventional lifestyles. Of course, there were times like yesterday when those two adorable urchins arrived on her doorstep that she would have given anything for a telephone to save her from the treacherous march from her place to the mansion next door. How much simpler her life would be now had she simply been able to make a call to the children's workaholic daddy without ever having to look directly into his hypnotic gray eyes. The color defied the artist in her to capture it on canvas.

Never alone in the solitude of her imagination, Ella was content spending her days in the long, comforting shadows of the Wind River Mountains. Some of her happiest moments had been spent rocking contentedly on her front porch, listening to the joyful trill of the meadowlarks' songs as she painted the world the way she thought it should be. Her new boss may have a veritable castle in comparison, but Ella was nonetheless hesitant to leave her own place behind. After years of thankless servitude, she thoroughly enjoyed the luxury of having no one to take care of but herself.

Remembering all the times she had given her heart to a needy family only to have them roughly return it when her indenture was up, Ella told herself not to get overly involved with Billy and Sarah. It wouldn't surprise her if their well-to-do papa didn't give up on Wyoming before the end of his first winter, soon tiring of the state's harsh climate, forced isolation and dearth of urbane culture. Her new neighbor's fancy furnishings suggested William Fawson Hawk III was more into highbrow society events and yuppie comforts than rodeos and ranching. Ella suspected that like many rich transplants, he considered the latter more a hobby than an actual profession.

Not that it mattered to her one way or the other. The extravagant salary he was offering her to take care of his children was enough to help Ella set aside any qualms about her "hottie" new boss. Haughty was more like it, she thought to herself, mentally engaging in an imaginary conversation with Phoebe, the long-time friend who introduced her to that latest college expression for an attractive member of the opposite sex.

Phoebe was certain to go wild over Hawk. Boy crazy since seventh grade, her best friend was still breaking her neck following any cute male butt that happened to sashay by. Secretly Ella suspected Phoebe had taken a college art course with her simply to ogle the nude male models who were paid to pose for the class. A hopeless romantic, Phoebe was one to create great love stories out of harmless flirtations and the most innocuous glances.

Depositing her treasured box of art supplies into the back of the pickup, Ella set about the task of gathering up the litter of abandoned kittens. Despite the affectionate petting they received beforehand, they mewled in protest at being confined to and transported inside a cardboard box. Though Ella doubted anyone would actually bother breaking in to her humble abode, she nonetheless locked the front door and said a silent farewell to her home. With a regretful sigh, she placed the kittens on the front seat of her pickup, tossed her suitcase in the back, and headed for her new job.

The distance between her cabin and Hawk's Red Feather Ranch was relatively short as the crow flies. Wearing tennis shoes, Ella could make the trek through aspen groves and crisscrossing creeks in approximately fifteen minutes. Unfortunately since roads were not engineered according to a crow's good sense, she was compelled to drive the perimeter of her few acres and around Hawk's vast pastureland. She rolled down the windows to cross-ventilate the aging pickup. She didn't mind the wind messing up her hair on such a glorious day as today.

The meadows clung tenaciously to the last green of the fading summer season. It wouldn't be long before the aspen leaves would be devouring the hillsides in fiery bursts of red and orange. Ella was sorely tempted to pull over and capture the way the morning light cast a celestial halo around Gannet Peak. The highest summit in Wyoming, it towered above the granite back of the Wind River Range. Ella loved hiding fantasy creatures in the backgrounds of her paintings. Squinting against the rose-colored sunrise, she could just make out a satyr's frosted beard in the snow that remained on the Peak all year long.

A black-and-white speckled kitten she'd dubbed Holstein crawled out of the nest of drowsy siblings and toppled over the edge of its box. Ella picked it up and set it on her lap with a gentle admonition not to interfere with the driving task at hand.

"Now that I'm back to punching a time clock," she told the kitten, "there's no time to tarry."

Filing the memory of that panoramic scene in her mind for future reference, she continued down the washboard road that led to the Red Feather Ranch. A half an hour later, Ella was standing on her employer's spacious front deck, pressing the doorbell. And pressing it again. And again. When both her finger and her patience wore out, expediency directed her to simply let herself in.

She was certain that she had not misunderstood either the day or the time they had agreed upon for beginning her employment. The instant she stepped inside it was apparent why no one had bothered answering the doorbell. It was impossible to hear anything over the television blaring out cartoons at full volume. She shook her head at the monstrous big-screen set. Why anyone would want a movie screen dominating their living space was beyond her understanding. Personally she considered television a major waste of time and was put off by the constant drone of commercialism trying to convince her that her wants and needs were one in the same.

Ella picked her way across a room littered with toys to shut the abandoned appliance off. Following the noise of a video game reverberating down the hallway, she proceeded to Hawk's den where she found him once again glued to his computer.

He needed a haircut, she noticed. His dark hair was beginning to curl over the collar of his expensive shirt. Standing safely in the open doorway, Ella was free to study him without his knowledge or permission. She had little fear he would feel her gaze upon him. It appeared the entire house could fall down around those football shoulders of his without him losing focus.

That such a gorgeous hunk was in actuality a computer nerd would no doubt disappoint Phoebe, but Ella wasn't about to argue with the facts before her. Or acknowledge the increase in her heart rate as she covertly admired her employer's physical attributes. The ability to concentrate entirely upon one's work was something Ella understood and respected. She had just never realized that business could hold the same all encompassing allure for someone as art did for her. Deciding it would be best not to disturb Hawk when he was so wrapped up in his work, she silently continued on with her search for Billy and Sarah.

Drawn to their playroom by the electronic sounds of alien destruction, Ella unearthed them at last. They were sitting slack-jawed in front of a video game, nimbly maneuvering their respective joysticks and mumbling incoherently.

"I think you've done your part to save the universe for today," Ella said, getting their attention by shutting the game off.

They reacted as if she had cut off their oxygen supply.

"We were in the middle of a game!" Billy protested, an unpleasant whine tingeing his voice.

"Yeah!" Sarah reiterated, placing her little hands defiantly on her hips.

Billy reached over to reactivate the game. He was perplexed when the screen remained blank. Swinging the disconnected cord around in her hand like a modern-day lariat, Ella was determined to let them both know from the get-go who was in charge.

"Hey!" they hollered.

"Straw!" she rejoined with a grin.

Determined to limit the amount of time the children spent in front of a glowing screen, Ella informed them both that she needed their help unpacking. They groaned. Sarah threatened to "tell my daddy on you" if Ella didn't plug the set back in immediately.

"Go ahead," Ella told her, not in the least nonplused. She wasn't about to be manipulated by two small children, no matter how precocious they were. Of course, she didn't want to start her tenure off with an angry confrontation either. Hoping to avert a power struggle, she tried distracting them from the crisis of the moment.

"I brought you both a surprise," she said.

Two pair of curious eyes studied her with sudden interest.

"What is it?" Billy wanted to know.

"A toy?" Sarah inquired.

"No, not a toy." Ella laughed, thinking of all the discarded playthings strewn throughout the house. Without giving it a thought, she plopped down on the floor beside them to meet them at eye level. "It looks to me like you have more than enough toys than are good for any boy or girl. Tell me, do you like animals?"

They both nodded their heads enthusiastically.

"What do you think about taking on the responsibility of a pet? A living, breathing creature that would be dependent on you for its care?"

"Really?" Sarah asked in delight.

"Really," Ella assured her, pushing a golden lock of the girl's disheveled hair away from her face. "That is, *if* you two think you're big enough and responsible enough to take care of them."

Unable to contain their inquisitiveness a moment longer, they jumped to their feet demanding to know what manner of creature their new nanny had brought them. Billy said he hoped it wasn't a fish because he'd had some of those once and they all had died on him. Grabbing Ella by both hands, they pulled her up from the floor. The next thing Ella knew, Billy was dragging her battered suitcase up the front steps and Sarah was helping bring her art supplies into her new bedroom. She didn't so much as have time to check out her new surroundings before they were pulling her back outside, demanding to see what was making all the noise in that curious cardboard box in the cab of her pickup.

Ella knew full well that she should have obtained Hawk's permission before bringing a litter of kittens into his home. She rationalized the oversight by telling herself every boy and girl should have a pet to love and care for. Besides, what would she have done had Hawk said no? She couldn't very well dump the kittens on somebody else's doorstep as had been done to her. Considering how much easier it often was to obtain forgiveness rather than permission, she planned on using the desperateness of Hawk's situation to smooth things over.

Just watching the children giggling and playing with their newfound friends made Ella feel better about her decision. She may not have been raised with all the financial advantages these children had, but before she died, her mother had cultivated Ella's imagination and planted the seeds of kindness in her daughter's heart. There was no denying that money could buy many material things, but one look at those children's excited faces reaffirmed something it couldn't procure. The joy received from a real live kitten was better any day of the week than all the video games in the world.

Hawk glanced at the clock on the wall in surprise. He couldn't believe he'd gotten so much pressing work done without the usual interruptions that had him pulling his hair out by the roots. Pushing himself away from the computer, he strained to hear the reassuring noise of his children at play—even if that meant they were bickering again. When nothing but the sound of silence reached his ears, his heart tightened in his chest. What was wrong? Where were his babies? And what in the world were they up to now?

Hawk checked his watch. The young woman he'd hired as their nanny should have been here quite some time ago. Though she had struck him as a flaky sort the instant he'd set eyes on her, something about her direct gaze, self-righteous attitude and firm grasp had given him the distinct impression that her word was good. The fact that her references had indeed checked out merely confirmed his gut feeling that she was a rare find. Where could she be?

He hurried from his office into the living room and was stopped by what he saw—or rather by what he didn't see. It took Hawk a moment to figure out what was different. The toys were picked up, the laundry was off the floor and the big-screen television set was off. Hawk found the children's bedrooms and playroom in a similar state of order. Since it seemed unlikely that a kidnapper would stop to tidy up, he could only assume that Ella had arrived like some fairy godmother to wave a wand over his life.

The calm for which he'd so often wished was nothing short of eerie as he realized that without his children this was what his life would be. Silent, still and empty.

Hawk suddenly felt the need to surround himself with the sound of his children's laughter. Where were they? Glancing out the front picture window, he spied them at last. With bright handkerchiefs tied to the end of sticks, they were marching dutifully to a spot of shade beneath the old apple tree. Trailing behind was a parade of kittens. One even had a tiny flag attached to its swishing tail. It was almost as cute as their new nanny's trim derriere swaying in time to the music they created with pots and pans and an old kazoo.

Hawk wished he had a camera handy to capture the moment on film. Sarah and Billy looked like little hobos following a red-haired pied piper. She was in the act of spreading a blanket upon the ground for this joyful, impromptu picnic. They all were smiling broadly, laughing and having a grand time. Something uncomfortably akin to jealousy twisted inside Hawk's guts at the sight. He hadn't witnessed such expressions of rapt fascination on his children's faces since well before their mother's funeral. Had he failed them so miserably that a virtual stranger could waltz in and steal their affection with little more than a sandwich and a bag of marshmallows?

And why hadn't anyone bothered asking him to partake in this makeshift celebration?

While Hawk felt deeply grateful to Ella for her skill and inventiveness in entertaining his children and cleaning up the weekend's accumulation of clutter, on a purely visceral level, he felt fear welling up inside the pit of his stomach as he studied his children's beaming faces through a plate glass window. He took a closer look at the amazing young woman he'd managed to hire to look after Billy and Sarah. In a pair of jeans and a pale lemon sweater with her thick russet tresses unfurled around her shoulders, she presented a much less ridiculous figure than she had the day before. Here was Gidget and Ann Margret and every adolescent boy's fantasy prom date all rolled into one.

The involuntary stirring in the lower part of his body at the sight of her falling down upon the blanket to instruct his children in the art of cloud gazing was tempered by a jolt of guilt. Why, she was but a child herself! Far too young and naive to have a grown father figure panting after her like some silly pup that didn't know any better. Like someone who hadn't already had his heart ripped out and stomped upon until it almost stopped beating entirely.

He hoped it hadn't been a mistake bringing Ella here. The truth of the matter was Hawk didn't need such a luscious complication in his life right now. Having buried his passion with his wife, he had no desire to resurrect it again. Certainly not with a younger woman in his employ.

A litter box was uppermost on Ella's list of supplies that she was going to pick up in town. She had survived the first night in Hawk's home, and though her employer had been clearly displeased that his new nanny came with a box of kittens, he hadn't insisted that either the kittens or Ella be put out. To have done so would have risked the wrath of his children who had promptly fallen in love with their new pets. Though Holstein and Sly remained loyally attached to Ella, Chin and Chilla were fickle creatures who seemed to instinctively understand which side of their bread was buttered with gourmet cat flavors. They purred with delight in the new masters' little arms, giving Ella a look that as much as said there would be no more Spartan table scraps in their future. Thank the gods of universal justice, their lives as paupers were over. Indeed, Hawk had instructed her to pick up all the amenities their new pets would need.

One white puff ball, dubbed Hissy Face, demanded her fair share of food without so much as a gracious exchange of allowing anyone to pick her up and pet her. If anyone so dared, she would unsheathe her claws from their velvet scabbards and spit in alarm. For some inexplicable reason Hissy Face affixed herself to the one person in the house who made it exceedingly clear that he wanted absolutely nothing whatsoever to do with her or any of her siblings. Hawk swore the beast purposely set out to trip him whenever he crossed a room. Ella assured him it was merely "puppy" love and advised him not to fight it.

At this choice of words, Hawk turned hooded gray eyes upon her. Ella seemed not in the least intimidated by his look of censure. She merely grinned as she stuffed his checkbook in the back pocket of a pair of cut off jeans that showed off the length and curve of legs that apparently remained stubbornly pale no matter how much they were exposed to the sun.

"Are you sure you trust me with several blank, signed checks?" she asked.

Hawk considered the question from a business perspective. If she ran off with his money or squandered it on luxuries for herself, it wouldn't be the first time someone had tried to take advantage of his generosity and his means. What was it about those wide emerald eyes of hers that encouraged Hawk to put his faith in this indomitably perky young woman?

"If I trust you with my children, how could I not entrust you with my money when one is so insignificant compared to the other?" he asked honestly.

Startled by the sincerity and wisdom with which Hawk had responded to her inquiry, all teasing left Ella's eyes. Had she so grievously misjudged him? She had been under the impression that he had been desperate enough that day she had stumbled into his life to hire anyone with a pulse. Perhaps the same instincts that made him an extraordinary businessman made him a good judge of character as well. It had never occurred to Ella that capitalists might be driven by anything other than a provable bottom line.

"I want you to get whatever you want at the store," Hawk told her, ignoring the look of surprise on her pretty face. She looked utterly enchanting with her glorious mane of russet hair pulled back and captured by a green ribbon that matched her eyes. "Please don't feel the need to pinch pennies. Buy whatever is convenient to stick in the oven. We're not picky eaters. Make things easy on yourself."

Ella fingered the coupons in her front pocket. Never before had she had carte blanche with someone else's money. She wasn't sure whether she was capable of shopping without mentally tallying the bill as she put each item into her cart.

"Go ahead and take my car," Hawk said, tossing her the keys.

Ella looked at him doubtfully. She had seen that expensive foreign job parked out front and wasn't convinced she wanted to be charged with such responsibility. Realizing that Hawk probably didn't think her rusty, old pickup was reliable enough transportation for his children, she bit her tongue. He was probably right. Ella's mechanic maintained the only thing holding the vehicle together was bailing wire and a prayer.

Reading the doubt upon her features, Hawk assured her, "Don't worry. I'm amply insured."

Ella gave him a grateful smile. His red sports car was parked out front. The epitome of opulence in sports cars, this particular model nonetheless held four comfortably. She loaded the children into their seats, buckled them safely in, and turned the ignition. It purred like one could only imagine Hissy Face might some day under perfect conditions. The seats were low to the ground and took some getting used to. Settling down into the butter-soft leather upholstery, Ella told herself that given half a chance she could easily adjust to such luxury.

Hawk walked out to the car and answered any questions Ella had about how the BMW sports car handled. Like a dream, she suspected. It didn't take long for Hawk to familiarize her with all the buttons and gadgets on the dashboard. As the children blew their father farewell kisses, Ella rolled down her window and tried to look at ease behind the wheel of a fifty-thousand-dollar vehicle.

Hawk thought she could have well posed for a glamour shot sitting behind the wheel looking as lovely and carefree as someone born to such extravagance. In her worn cutoffs and sleeveless cotton shirt, she looked the fresh-faced all-American girl. That her makeup was minimal simply added to her allure. Physical attributes aside, Hawk decided, it was Ella's animated response to life in general that made her so appealing. Looking back on it, he couldn't believe he had found her less than stunning the first time he'd set eyes on her. Just remembering her ragtag appearance of flaming hair and righteous outrage that day was enough to make him smile.

Glad to see the genuine affection between Hawk and his children, Ella returned his smile. Having spent time in any number of homes, she knew how truly rare such demonstrations of love were. Indeed, experience had taught her that sometimes the most elegant homes housed the coldest families.

Nonetheless Ella could not keep the look of chastisement from her face as Hawk gave his children twenty dollars each for whatever "trinkets" they might find on their excursion in town. She had definite ideas about spoiling children and teaching them the value of hard work by attaching it to earnings. It was her considered opinion that most parents needed to spend less money and more time on their children. While it may be spare change for Hawk, the forty bucks with which he'd just parted was more than Ella had in her own purse at the moment. Luckily, her employer had given her a check in advance for her services, and she was as eager to put that substantial amount in the bank before any of her bills came due.

The thought of pulling up in front of Phoebe's apartment in this extravagant contraption caused the corners of her mouth to tug into a smile. All she was missing was glass slippers and an elegant ball gown to complete the picture. As Hawk placed a parting kiss atop Sarah's golden head, a careless thought flitted through Ella's mind as she imagined him stopping by her open window, bending down, and kissing her farewell, too. The thought sent blood pumping through her body in hot spurts that caused her to blush unaccountably.

When Hawk did saunter over to her window to offer his parting remarks, Ella was aware that her face rivaled her hair in its damnable shade of red. His suggestion that she pick up some sunscreen while in town only caused her to glow a deeper crimson. She hoped he was distracted from the glow by his children hollering, "See ya later alligator."

To which, Hawk dutifully responded, "In a while crocodile."

He stood in the driveway a long time, staring after them, eating the dust of their departure. He wasn't quite sure how she managed to do it, but somehow Ella was able to make even a trip to the grocery store into an exciting adventure. He used to look forward to the one day a week when the previous nanny had taken the children off the ranch and out of his hair for an afternoon of shopping. Rather than that familiar sense of relief, Hawk trudged back to his workstation feeling oddly bereft.

The house was blessedly quiet. Nothing was stopping him from catching up on a truckload of work this afternoon. Nothing but the sense that he was being left out of his children's lives and the vague memory of once upon a time knowing how to have fun himself.

Three

Ella quickly discovered that shopping with money was a whole lot more fun than her usual forays into the discount world. Under normal circumstances she left shops feeling emotionally beaten and harried. What a change to point her nose disdainfully in the air as she passed the "day old" bread and loaded her cart full with what she considered to be extravagant items. The foremost among them was a big bottle of bubble bath and a very small bottle of the most sensual perfume she had ever smelled. Not wanting to give her employer any reason to find her unworthy of his trust, Ella paid for these two indulgences out of her own pocket. The rest was going to bills and straight into her college fund.

Her first night at Red Feather Ranch had felt like a stay in a sumptuous hotel. Compared to her old feather bed, the new mattress and springs in her room were heaven. Next to the forced air heater which would keep her toasty

warm on long winter nights, the undisputed best thing
about her new living quarters was the attached bathroom
complete with a shower and tub, which she wantonly had
filled to the brim with steamy hot water. It had been in
that deliciously relaxing bath that Ella had decided to add
bubble bath to her shopping list.

Ah, the comforts that so many people dared take for
granted, she thought to herself taking an appreciative sniff
of the peach bubble bath she had selected from the store
shelf. Still, old habits die hard, and so it was that Ella
could not actually bring herself to buy the myriad of expensive gourmet brands that she had always fancied. She
did, however, yield to the children in their choice of cold
cereals with "fabulous prizes" inside, as well succumbing
to the charm of a bouquet of fresh-cut flowers for the
kitchen table. They would make a lovely still life if she
ever found the time to capture it on canvas. Before leaving, she gave Sarah and Billy each a gleeful turn on the
antique horse that had sat at the front of the grocery store
for as long as Ella could remember. Lurching drunkenly
in place, poor old Bullet bore the weight of multiple gen-
erations upon its worn saddle. He stoically endured the
bit attached to the real leather reins which youngsters
pulled on while slapping his paint-flecked rump urging
him to gallop. For the price of a single penny, it was
assuredly the best ride in town.

Just as Ella had feared, the children blew their money
on useless junk that she knew would likely be broken or
discarded before they even got back home. Her suggestions that they either save their money for a big ticket
item or invest in rainy day art supplies was met with all
the resistance two preschoolers with forty dollars between
them could muster. In the end, Ella had surrendered to
their wishes, reminding herself that it was neither her

money nor they her children. A somber thought reinforced by past experiences reminded her to keep her emotional distance lest her tender heart be hurt again.

The first thing she did upon depositing their purchases into the trunk of the car was stop by Phoebe's house. Both the fancy car and her friend's good fortune overwhelmed the lively blonde. Phoebe purported that the only people who owned such cars were old goats trying to reclaim their youth and as such, she remained skeptical as to the owner's real identity. As they all piled into the BMW sports car and headed to the Dairy Palace for ice cream, Phoebe made Ella promise to introduce her to the "hottie" aristocrat her best friend claimed as her boss. If indeed William Fawson Hawk III was too stodgy and business oriented for Ella's freewheeling taste, Phoebe said she wasn't above falling in love with a rich, handsome tycoon.

Before stopping for ice cream, they hung a couple of Mains on Lander's major thoroughfare with their state-of-the-art stereo system turned up loud enough to make the children squeal with delight as they joined in on loud off-key choruses. Parking the car away from other vehicles that might cause a scratch or door ding, they stopped for ice cream. Outside, the sun was warm and the air pleasantly still. Sitting beneath the yellow-and-white awning of the old-fashioned ice cream parlor watching the traffic go by added to the charm of what seemed to be a town that time forgot.

Phoebe pasted a disgusted expression on her face. "One of the horses in this two-horse burg must have died last night."

She made no secret of the fact that she was looking forward to shaking the familiar dust of her hometown from her feet, the sooner the better. Once she got her computer certification from the nearby community college, Phoebe Tyler was bound for more glamorous destinations. Convinced of her friend's artistic talents she took every opportunity to encourage Ella to come along with her. After all, discovery by the art world in Lander, Wyoming, was about as likely as winning the state lottery—odds lessened considerably by the fact that the state didn't have one.

Savoring her strawberry ice cream, Ella refused to be ruffled on such a glorious day as this. A country girl at heart, she felt no need to run off to the big city looking for fame and fortune. This quaint little town was as cosmopolitan as she needed, nestled as it was at the base of the mountains that held her heart. She wiped matching chocolate ice cream mustaches from the children's faces with a napkin. They didn't put up much of a fight when Ella announced it was time to go home. All in all, they seemed to have had a wonderful time sampling the sweetness of the day.

Promising to see each other at their art class Wednesday night, the two old friends departed. The sun was sinking low in the sky when Ella turned on a soothing CD in hopes of combating all the sugar racing through the children's systems. It wasn't long before their heads were bobbing and they were out, soundly napping for the duration of the ride home. She found them undeniably beautiful in their sleep. Billy with his thick mop of dark hair and open gray eyes was the very image of his father physically, though Ella doubted whether Hawk had ever displayed his son's wonderfully mischievous, playful nature. More than likely, William Fawson Hawk III had been a serious and intent child whose favorite pastime was a Monopoly game. Ella assumed Sarah got her pretty blond curls and blue eyes from her mother. Having glanced at the pictures on the mantel in their home, she ascertained that the gorgeous creature enshrined there had to be their mother. Or a movie star.

Those pale reflections of what Mrs. William Hawk had been in the flesh were chilling reminders of how dearly missed she was by every member of this fragile family. And how hopelessly plain and boring she must seem to them. Despite Phoebe's determination to make her life into a fairy tale, Ella knew better than to waste her time dreaming of men like Hawk ever paying her the slightest bit of attention as anything other than a paid employee. Sighing, she squinted against the setting sun and promised to buy herself a pair of funky sunglasses on her next trip to town.

Having had a whole, rare uninterrupted day, Hawk was surprised how difficult it had been to concentrate in all that solitude. After an hour or two of truly productive work, he found himself actually turning on the television set just to have the comfort of its droning noise in the background. Though a poor substitute for the sound of his children's chatter, it was notably better than the silence for which he had so foolishly been longing. At odd times he would look up from his computer screen as if straining to catch pieces of conversation between his absent children and their new nanny. He had purposely positioned his desk against a blank wall so as to minimize distractions, but after a miserable lunch of potato chips and pop, decided to move it next to the window so as to have a better view of the backyard. Images of Ella casually dressed in cutoffs came unbidden to him throughout the day, disrupting his concentration and his peace of mind. He certainly hoped she took part of her advance paycheck and invested in more suitable attire.

Hawk became so bored and lonely that he actually sought out Hissy Face's dubious company as comfort. He received a nasty scratch on his arm for his efforts. He wasn't sure why he secretly liked the cursed animal— other than the fact that he felt somehow connected to a fellow creature who desperately wanted to be loved but was afraid of allowing anyone to do so.

By the time his dust-covered BMW sports car pulled into the driveway later that evening, Hawk was unaccountably irritated by the sight of three sunburned beauties bearing cold burritos and exciting tales of the day's adventures. Despite Ella's assurances that she was perfectly capable of bringing in the groceries herself, he allowed her to carry only a couple of smaller bags. She offered to heat up Hawk's dinner in the microwave while the children filled him in on all the details of their day.

As excited as they were, one would have thought they'd just returned from an amusement park instead of a jaunt into town. It had been a long time since his children had displayed such enthusiasm for sharing much of anything with Hawk, and he was happy to take advantage of the opportunity to get close to them. He couldn't shake the feeling that they somehow distrusted him after their mother's death. Not that they blamed him for her demise or anything so sinister, it was just that it seemed a stranger had waltzed into their lives trying to take their mother's place. And doing an abysmal job of it.

Hawk deeply regretted the way he had so neatly compartmentalized his life before Lauren's death. That was as much her choice as it had been his. Still, that knowledge was of little solace to a man trying to piece his life back together like some gigantic three dimensional puzzle strewn over years of mistakes. Though not a particularly warm woman, Lauren had loved her children in her own way, setting them up to have the best of everything from designer clothing to prestigious preschools. Her insistence that Hawk's primary obligation to his family was to provide them an income adequate to support her considerable tastes was something that had caused him a good deal of emotional turmoil in the past as well as the present.

Lauren had been from the kind of old and, unfortunately, dwindling money lines that understood children were to be molded into a commodity to advance one's standing in society. To her credit, she had done an admirable job sorting Billy and Sarah into fashionably regimented activities that ensured they caused their parents as little trouble as possible. At the time of her death she had been determined that their children would attend one of the most touted boarding schools available.

That Hawk had hired a nanny who not only played with them but also encouraged them to get dirty would have surely horrified his elegant wife. As would Ella's choice of casual attire and the unabashed exuberance with which she attacked each day. Hawk smiled. Because she was quite the opposite of his departed wife, his parents would love Ella. In the brief time the children had spent with their grandparents while Hawk was getting his life in order, they had begun shedding layers of inhibition. Like Ella, his parents didn't prescribe to Lauren's "children should be seen but not heard" philosophy.

As tempting as it would have been to leave Billy and Sarah in their grandparents' care indefinitely, Hawk didn't want to strain their failing health any more than absolutely necessary. Besides, he truly wanted to be part of his children's life. Sadly, ever since he'd uprooted them and transplanted them to the Wyoming backcountry, where he himself had grown up so long ago, he'd gotten the feeling that they'd rather be anywhere but with him on a full-time basis. Perhaps they had simply become far too comfortable with the good-time dad image he'd portrayed for so long—that of the absent father who showed up between mergers to shower them with gifts, hoping to make up for the time he couldn't afford to give them. Such tactics had extracted a heavy toll on his marriage as well as on Hawk's relationship with his children. There was so much he regretted, so much he blamed on himself alone.

"Anyone up for a Candy Land game?" Ella asked, carrying a huge bowl of freshly popped buttered popcorn into the room along with a platter of reheated burritos for Hawk.

Immediately the children began clearing a space at the table. Famished, Hawk dug in.

"May I play?" he asked, halfway through his first burrito.

Startled by the request, the children looked at him as if he were a complete stranger to them.

"Certainly," Ella interjected into the noticeable silence. "But I have to warn you, I am the Candy Land champion of the world."

The children booed, promising to best both of the adults present. Ella was pleased that Hawk had asked to join in. She found him to be surprisingly patient in playing the child-centered board game. He really had a nice smile when he used it. Something about the curve of those sensuous lips made her go quite soft inside, and she quickly bent her head over the game when Hawk caught her gawking at him.

Ella was impressed by the fact that he was trying so hard to connect with his children. Her mother maintained that Ella's father had been a magician. When she told him that she was pregnant, he disappeared. Ella had to admire a man who cared enough to stick around and see his children through the tough times. She found herself wondering if it wasn't so much that William Fawson Hawk III was aloof, as he was simply ill at ease in the role in which fate had cast him. She wondered if his gorgeous wife had ever included him in such simple pastimes. The thought of the four of them nestled in front of a roaring fire made Ella's stomach twist. Doing her best to dismiss the fear that she would never find such cozy contentment in a relationship, Ella turned over a card that allowed her to skip way ahead in the game.

Throwing a wink in Hawk's direction, she said, "I told you I was lucky."

A flicker of something dangerous danced in slate-colored eyes. "I think we're the lucky ones," he told her.

Ella cursed herself for blushing like a schoolgirl with a crush.

"You are very lucky to have each other," she said, meaning it.

Despite her efforts to lose to one of the younger players, Ella was the undisputed winner of the evening. The children scampered off to brush their teeth as the grownups promised to put away the game. As she was clearing the board, her hand inadvertently brushed against Hawk's. She flinched as if she had just been shocked by a stun gun. The tingling in her hand extended all the way up her arm, settling deep inside her in the most private places.

"There's no reason for you to be afraid of me," Hawk chided softly. He blithely attempted to cover his lie with the old hackneyed expression that had been a favorite of his mother's. "I don't bite, you know."

Oh, that you would! Ella thought to herself.

Embarrassed by the direction her thoughts were taking, she reminded herself that her handsome employer was no more attracted to her than he was to the mail carrier. Poor old Mrs. Hennerson was nearing the age of forced retirement and not a minute too soon if you asked any of the folks whose mailboxes she had plowed over because she was too vain to wear her glasses.

Though instinct bid her to bite her tongue, Ella plunged bravely onward. "What makes you think I'm afraid of you?" she asked, scooping the multicolored markers into her hand and clenching them tightly.

Reaching over his corner of the table, Hawk brushed a silky lock of hair away from her forehead. "The way your eyes widen whenever I get too close. The way you act as if my touch were toxic. The way you skitter away from me when I come too near."

"That's ridiculous!" she protested. Her voice sounded shrill and loud to her own ears.

"Is it?"

Hawk placed an index finger beneath her stubborn chin and forced her to lift her gaze from the floor to look him straight in the eyes. The heat radiating from his eyes rivaled the flame of his touch. An embarrassing little gasp escaped Ella's lips.

"Of course," she said, trying to make light of the fact that her pulse was bounding out of control. She had the most unaccountable urge to unbutton Hawk's shirt and touch her palms to the dark pelt of hair that peeked out of his open collar.

"Why would someone like me be afraid of you?" Ella asked. She didn't need a mirror to remind her how unlikely it was that someone as drop-dead gorgeous as Hawk would be interested in someone as plain as she.

Falling into eyes the delicate color of budding aspen leaves, Hawk smiled enigmatically, lowering his head to hers. "Because, Miss McBride, you are far too sweet for your own good."

There was no doubt about it. He was going to kiss her. Ella trembled in anticipation. The unadulterated lust glimmering in his eyes made her feel suddenly as beautiful as a princess in a story of her own making. Her eyelids fluttered shut. Every cell in her body radiated heat and desire as her lips parted in anticipation.

His mouth was demanding as it settled over her lips. Rather than pulling away, Ella allowed herself to revel in the hot urgency of his kiss. She had been kissed before but never like this. Assailed by the tender crushing force that opened her lips in a gasp, she allowed Hawk's tongue entrance to what was surely her very soul.

He kissed her with a thoroughness that made her weak and left her wanting. Woozy, she did not fight the passion making her knees wobble and her heart palpitate like crazy. Hawk splayed his hands across her back and drew her closer. Too shocked to resist, she wound her arms around his neck and held on for dear life, succumbing to the temptation to give just as good as she got. The intensity of her reaction evoked a delicious masculine groan somewhere deep in his throat, assuring a brazen Ella that he was as addicted to her kisses as she to his.

As her lips softened beneath his kisses, a surge of womanly power rocked her body. Held tightly against his hard planes in a grip both strong and commanding, she indulged her senses in the feel of his masculine body. Obviously he found time enough to actually use all those expensive exercise machines in his personal gym just off the playroom. He was all muscle and sinew. Sighing with pleasure, she molded her rounded curves around his hard angles. Lost in a swirl of sensual pleasure, her eyes fluttered closed.

When she opened them again, it was to discover that Hawk had stepped out of her embrace and disappeared just as neatly as her father had once upon a time.

Four

Ella stood over her sink for a long time that night trying to wash away the tingling where Hawk's touch had left its indelible mark. It was the epitome of foolishness to think he had stopped kissing her out of some noble, misguided intention. One look at the freckled-faced, red-haired image in the mirror set her straight on that account. Phoebe could maintain all she wanted that her beauty was unique unto itself, but Ella knew what that delicate phrasing really meant. She was one ugly duckling who was not about to turn into a swan anytime soon.

It was no wonder that Hawk had had such little trouble backing off before anything seriously compromising happened between them. Ella knew she should be grateful to him for his restraint. The last thing she needed to do was risk her job over a foolish fling with the boss. Not only wouldn't it be good for her, it would devastate the children. If either of them had happened upon that kiss, they would surely feel betrayed. That they loved and missed their mother was never far from Ella's mind. The fact that her well-honed sense of self-preservation hadn't immediately kicked in made her wonder how it might feel to be dealt with as a sexual being for a change instead of as a servant with a strong back and a big heart. Sighing, she patted her face dry with a big, fluffy towel and crawled into her luxuriously firm bed.

She might as well have been resting on a mattress of nails. Hawk had gotten under her skin—and that irritant proved to be far more substantial than the single pea placed under a mountain of bedding to bedevil that fair princess in one of her favorite children's stories. In a futile attempt to get comfortable, Ella flounced her pillows, kicked out the hospital corners of her sheets, and finally succumbed to the lure of her sketch pad. By the wee hours of the morning she had captured a smiling, gray-eyed demon on paper. Whether he would prove to be a knight or a beast in one of her stories was yet to be determined.

When the alarm jolted her into consciousness a few short hours later, Ella was determined to treat last night's indiscretion as nothing more than just that. If Hawk didn't mind pretending that those earth-shattering kisses had never happened, she was willing to try repressing the memory as well. Of course, the fact that just thinking about it set her to quivering made a lie out of her resolve. Demonstrating her immunity to him was going to be the challenge of the day. Rather, of the duration of her employment.

It had been a mistake to kiss her. Hawk knew it the instant that reckless urge seized him. What he hoped might pass as a harmless "thanks for taking such good care of my children" peck of appreciation had awakened in him the kind of longing that he thought he had buried long ago. Hawk had kissed his fair share of women, and not a one of them had stirred in him the wild abandon that Ella had. Never would he have guessed that the red-haired Mary Poppins he'd hired on the spur of the moment could resurrect in him such powerful feelings as easily as she coaxed smiles from his children.

Children, he reminded himself roughly, who meant more to him than anything else in this world. He couldn't afford to jeopardize their happiness by scaring away the best thing that had happened to them since their mother had passed away. Hawk prided himself on making the kind of carefully considered decisions that had jettisoned him from the working middle class, up the corporate ladder, and eventually landed him the CEO position of his own lucrative business. He could see no excuse for the kind of stupidity that had him groping a perfectly delightful young creature last night and risking her willingness to remain in his employment.

No excuse other than a pair of kaleidoscope eyes that made him feel like they held the secret of happiness within their sea-green depths.

Lauren had been certain that happiness could be bought with money and status. Consequently, she had died searching for something more than Hawk could give her with an unlimited checking account and a promise of more money than she could ever spend. The taste of failure coated Hawk's mouth with regret. Feeling that his inability to keep his wife happy had placed her at the wrong place at the wrong time, Hawk couldn't help feeling partially responsible for her death. Images of her beautiful body mutilated in a car wreck haunted him yet.

That a vibrant young woman had jump-started his heart with the most disturbing kiss of his life was no reason to toss aside his guilt, not to mention everything he'd worked so hard to achieve. He was too old and jaded to compound his mistake by chasing silly dreams. Sensible single men with children and responsibilities and businesses to run weren't supposed to succumb to such foolishness until they hit their midlife crisis. At thirty-four Hawk felt only pity for those men of thickening bodies and balding pates who openly pursued younger women trying to recapture their youth. How foolish they looked racing down life's highway in a new convertible with their Rogaine solution and Viagra pills stashed in the glove box.

Given that sober line of thought, Hawk knew he should have been pleased to see Ella dressed the next morning in a baggy sweatshirt and jeans. Instead, her precautions to hide all those luscious curves only amused him. She wasn't fooling him one whit with that plain Jane routine. Having felt her body pressed against his, Hawk knew exactly what was concealed beneath all that excess material.

"Good morning," he said as lightly as if nothing more had passed between them than the aroma of bacon cooking on the stove.

"Good morning," Ella replied evenly, pretending her body hadn't reacted to his presence in the kitchen with an electrical charge that almost caused her to knock the skillet off the burner. She might have convincingly pulled it off, too, had she not been engulfed in a head-to-toe blush. It was a good thing the knives were put up high out of the children's reach or she might well have used one to open up a vein in embarrassment.

"Need any help?" Hawk asked.

"No!" The word left Ella's mouth like a bullet. "I'm fine," she added as an afterthought. "But thanks for the offer."

Seeing the laughter lurking in the corners of his gray

eyes, Ella backed away from the hot stove and inched her way down the kitchen counter until she reached the silverware drawer.

"You know, you're making me feel like a monster," Hawk said in reference to her blatant attempt at putting distance between them. He stepped closer and effectively pinned her against the counter.

A bittersweet ache settled into the center of Ella's being. The sexual tension between them sizzled hotter than the bacon on the stove. Although he worked at home in the backwoods of Wyoming, Hawk never came to the breakfast table unshaven. Having a decided preference for clean-shaven men, Ella thought it spoke highly of his self-discipline. He was close enough that she could see droplets of water from his morning shower clinging to his thick, dark hair. She breathed deeply of his uniquely masculine scent. A subtle blend of soap and musk, it stirred in her memories of the intimacy that had left her completely befuddled the night before.

"Would it help ease your worries if I apologized for kissing you last night?"

The question caught Ella off guard. In truth, she would have preferred he apologize for disappearing without a word to her after getting her so hot and bothered. She was tempted to graciously nod her head and get on with the business of stirring the pancake mix, miserable in the knowledge that it was as easy for this man to forget her kisses as he would leave a gratuity for good service.

"No matter what her station in life, a lady usually doesn't like to hear a man say he's sorry for kissing her," she said, looking him in the eye and speaking more primly than she had intended.

Startled by her honesty, Hawk crooked an eyebrow at her. Ella McBride was the most deliciously unpredictable creature he'd ever met. Even the funny, stilted way she had of stating things was unique. He had expected a sigh of relief and a stiff, formal acceptance of the olive branch which he'd offered. Instead she faced him down with a spatula and the most refreshing sincerity he'd encountered in years.

"What do you suggest we do then?" he asked, a smile toying with the corners of his mouth. "Would silverware at ten paces be fitting?"

The last thing Ella had expected was for his sense of humor to make an appearance. Having alternately cast him as a gruff businessman and a computer geek, she hadn't actually realized he had interpersonal skills that extended beyond a boardroom. Grateful for anything to lessen the tension between them, she brandished a spatula in his handsome face.

"I prefer steak knives myself," she parried, thinking how appropriate it would be to use it to cut out her heart, cook it up and serve it to her boss on a proverbial silver platter. "But I doubt you want to expose your children to unnecessary bloodshed, so I suppose that's out of the question."

"Definitely," Hawk agreed, wrinkling his forehead in mock deliberation. "Perhaps if you would be willing to call a truce, I'd offer to set the table."

Ella accepted the terms of their cease-fire with a laugh, and Hawk reached around her to open the silverware drawer. The hand that inadvertently brushed up against her waist acted as an electrical conduit holding her riveted in place. Scorched by the flame of desire dancing in those dove-gray eyes, Ella quickly twisted around to hide her own emotions from Hawk's scrutiny.

The lightest touch of his arms against her body as she turned away was enough to set her imagination sailing for erotic destinations. The thought of his arms wrapped around her waist...of his big, masculine hands caressing her breasts...of stepping back and cuddling her body against his in a fit as perfect as the two spoons she lifted out of the silverware drawer....

"You smell good," he told her, tucking a strand of hair behind her ear. For the life of him he didn't know why being threatened with a spatula had sent such unruly images racing through his mind.

The spoons clattered back in the drawer.

"Mmmmph," Ella mumbled, feeling a fool from the roots of her hair to the tips of her toenails. "It's maple syrup."

Lauren preferred Poison by Christian Dior perfume. Hawk had always found the name of that perfume rather unnerving. Maple syrup was far sweeter, though at the moment he wasn't so sure it wasn't infinitely more dangerous. If Ella had actually dabbed some behind her ear, he would gladly volunteer to lick it off. The errant thought poleaxed him. He had no idea how it could have materialized in a brain so consumed by business, fatherhood and a concentrated effort to forget anything that reminded him of Lauren.

Remembering the truce they had struck, Hawk removed his hands from the edges of the marble countertop—away from the fascinating creature who blushed so charmingly whenever he came too near.

"What smells?" asked Billy, wrinkling up his nose as he entered the room. His pajamas dragged on the floor.

Indeed, the bacon, forgotten on the stove, had turned a dark shade of brown that even the cats were likely to find unsuitable to their newly refined palates. Without thinking to grab a hot pad, Ella made a dive for the skillet.

Hawk's hand encircled her wrist and held her away from danger.

She hastened to apologize, parroting the words that had once preceded a beating she had received in a foster home. "I'm so sorry. There's no excuse for wasting food like that. Please take it out of my wages."

Hawk was disturbed by the terror lacing her voice. "Don't be silly," he said, grabbing a dishcloth from the counter and taking the skillet by the handle. He proceeded to dump the entire contents into the garbage.

"We'll just let this soak in the sink for a while and not give it another thought. Besides, it's as much my fault as yours. I've been in your way."

Ella had been in homes where such an oversight on her part was not treated as lightly. That Hawk considered this a little thing hardly worthy of concern made her feel a sense of gratitude toward him. Every day she was beginning to see more depth to this man. It had been far easier to think of him as a dictatorial, corporate father more concerned with business than with the raising of his children.

This was the man whom she had overheard tucking his children in and reading them a nighttime story. The man whose murmured "Sweet dreams" before he shut off their lights had turned her insides to mush. His kindness in such a small matter as a charred breakfast put a lump in her throat.

She gave him a grateful look, then turning to Billy asked, "Would you like to help me whip up a batch of pancakes? I'm quite an accomplished artist with pancake batter. Just tell me what kind of animal you want, and I'll do my best to make you an original edible creation."

Billy didn't have to think long. "A kitty," he told her without the slightest hint of skepticism in his voice that she couldn't make good on the deal.

"Okay, now run ask Sarah what she wants," Ella told him, eager to put her talents to use in the kitchen and forget the disaster smoldering in the garbage. She turned on the overhead fan, knowing that it was certain to take a while to get the stench out of the kitchen.

"Aren't you going to ask what I want?" Hawk queried.

The quiet power of his voice burned like whiskey on a cold day. Ella found herself foolishly hoping that he might want more from her than baby-sitting services. Her palms were so sweaty that she was afraid to pick up another kitchen utensil for fear of dropping it. Caught in the vortex of those amazing eyes of his, she answered his question with one of her own.

"And just what *do* you want?" she whispered, unable to keep the hesitancy from her voice.

Or the expectation.

"A bear."

Her forehead wrinkled in confusion.

"Can you make my pancake in the shape of a bear?" Hawk asked.

Noticing that there was not a trace of guile upon his aristocratic face, Ella wiped her hands on her jeans and shot him a haughty look. How dare he toy with her like a mere child! Despite her apparent lack of sophistication, Ella's little girl days had ended long before they should have.

She decided to treat Hawk like one of the cantankerous customers that frequented the Watering Hole. "A teddy bear or a grizzly?" she asked, somehow making it sound like a question from a personality quiz in one of those women's magazines lining checkout counters across the country.

"I prefer teddies," Hawk told her.

Ella wondered if he was deliberately trying to evoke an

image of sexy lingerie in her mind. She pretended that the timbre of his voice was not vibrating deep inside her, not plucking the chords of some ancient instrument hidden away from conscious awareness.

"A teddy bear it'll be then," she said, feigning an aloofness she did not feel.

Both Hawk and Ella looked relieved when Sarah walked through the door, climbed up on the stool at the marbled kitchen island and placed her order. She wanted her pancake in the shape of a monkey, thank you very much.

Ten minutes later they were all sitting down to eat breakfast sans bacon. Ella set their plates before them with a flourish. Before they could take a bite, she regretfully informed them that her artistry was simply too praiseworthy to actually eat. Indeed, on each platter was a recognizable creature: a kitten for Billy, a monkey with a funny tail for Sarah, and for their father a huge teddy bear with chocolate chips for eyes.

"Delicious," he assured her with a wink that made it difficult for her to swallow her own breakfast.

Hawk was surprised how eager his children were to assist her with chores. By the time the breakfast dishes were put away, she had cajoled them into making their beds and putting on their play clothes all in record time so they could all go on a nature walk and give their father "some peace and quiet." When transferred from the office to the home, Hawk's own personal style of management had more frequently led to tears on his children's part and frustration on his. He had to give credit where credit was due. Their new nanny simply had a knack for making the mundane fun.

Why that left him feeling so damned inadequate was not something Hawk wanted to spend much time overanalyzing. That this young woman could magically get the children to do their chores without engaging in a full-blown war was something he should appreciate, not resent. Just as the fact that Ella's beauty seemed to grow on him with each passing day should have brought pleasure rather than distress.

The self-control for which Hawk was so famous seemed to have abandoned him. One minute he was reproving himself for being inferior to Ella as a caretaker to his own children, and the next he was kissing her senseless. Not repeating that mistake was proving harder than he expected. Ever since Hurricane Ella had blown into his life, Hawk's emotions had been all mixed up. It was as disconcerting to find her so incredibly appealing in a baggy sweatshirt as it was to discover how much he disliked the quiet in the house whenever Ella took the children on another adventure just so he could concentrate on business. It struck him odd that he had all the money, but that Ella had all the fun. And that his children seemed to prefer her company to his.

Considering all that he'd sacrificed for them, it wasn't fair.

Why he missed the children's raucous presence underfoot was something that left him scratching his head in dismay. A week ago he had been so discombobulated by the demands of single fatherhood and running his own corporation that he was considering giving up on his whole elaborate scheme of reuniting and healing his family beneath the wide-open spaces of Wyoming's pristine sky. For a man so adept at running an amazingly successful business, Hawk found he was all thumbs when it came to getting his own children to comply with his wishes without some unpleasant power play occurring.

As much as Hawk appreciated what Ella was trying to

do by taking the children outside and getting them out of
his hair so he could concentrate on his work, he also felt
a tad resentful of being deprived of their presence for such
long stretches at a time. The silence in their absence settled around his heart like a heavy fog whenever he found
himself alone in that huge, custom-built house. He wondered if Lauren had felt such heaviness of solitude those
long years when he had labored so hard to make his business a success, if his absence hadn't been a contributing
factor to her death.

Determined to win back a permanent place in his children's hearts, Hawk promised not to let business consume
him as it had before. His presence was going to have to
be more than merely physical if they were ever to grow
into the kind of family he wanted them to become. Thus
it was that he decided to observe Ella's easy camaraderie
with the same kind of resolve that had helped him pirate
several successful, albeit hostile business takeovers. All
he had to do was watch and learn.

Hawk could come up with no appropriate business anal-
ogy by which to compare Ella McBride. Watching her
was more like stargazing—a dizzying exercise in the per-
ception of universal forces coming together in youth and
exuberance and amazing sensitivity. The fact that she
seemed to grow prettier each day didn't hurt his eyes any
either.

Hair that once had seemed to him too red and wild to
ever fit into his idea of refined beauty was beginning to
evoke in him a longing to sample its fiery fiber against
his own flesh. Unbidden throughout the day, images of
fiery copper spread out upon his own pillow flashed
through his mind, and he would upbraid himself for having such careless thoughts. He couldn't help but compare
Ella's earthy beauty to that of Lauren's cultivated ele-

gance. His wife's blond sophistication and blue blood had made for a nice trophy at his elbow, but all that golden allure had proven very cold in bed. From what Hawk had sampled of Ella's kisses, he suspected that she could be stroked into a volcanic display of passion that would rock a man off balance for a lifetime.

Hawk was delighted to hear the front door bang open with the return of his family. Suddenly feeling more contented and productive than he had all day, Hawk continued working at his computer station for another fifteen minutes before using his stomach as a pretense for getting a snack and sneaking through the other room. He wanted to see how Ella was keeping his two cherubs so unusually quiet without the aid of television.

In the middle of his living room Hawk found Ella bent over an ironing board that had been standing against the washroom wall for what he assumed was decoration. The last time anyone had actually ironed for him was his own mother. Lauren wouldn't have known one end of an ironing board from another. In fact, she would have turned up her pretty nose at the thought of ever doing such a labor-intensive task herself. Just the smell alone of the hot iron and the steam rising from beneath it brought back memories of his childhood. Hawk's mother had maintained that ironing was an act of love to show her family how much she cherished them.

The children were gathered about Ella as if she were performing a magic act rather than some taxing, ordinary chore. Methodically moving the iron back and forth, she wove them a story. From an observer's point of view, it seemed to Hawk that the act of ironing in itself helped unloose the creative flow from somewhere deep inside Ella. Her face took on the removed, rapt look of someone channeling from the heavens above.

Hawk found himself drawn into the story she told. It was an enchanting tale of a dragon that had lost his taste for saccharine maidens and sought instead double bacon cheeseburgers and fries. Every so often, Ella would punctuate her story with a shot of steam from the iron, purposely creating the impression of a dragon in the near vicinity.

Leaning up against the doorway, Hawk studied the scene with a professional eye. How she managed to make drudgery exciting was something he wished he could bottle. Ella seemed genuinely interested in the children's feedback at the conclusion of the story. Hawk found it curious that she would seek their input.

"Make up another one," Sarah demanded, startling Hawk with the possibility that Ella might have devised such a clever, entertaining story all on her own. Fantasy held little allure for the business world, but it did for anyone wanting to hold a child's attention. An apt student, Hawk was willing to learn whatever he could from this creative, free spirit.

"Bravo!" he said at the story's conclusion.

When Ella looked up and discovered him leaning against the doorsill, she blushed a lovely shade of pink. Why it pleased Hawk to have such an effect upon her was nothing he cared to ponder right at the moment, but there was no denying the rush of gratification that coursed through his body at her obvious awareness of his proximity.

"With the children's help," she said, making sure to include them in the process and give them credit for their input into the story she polished. "Telling stories is a hobby of mine."

Ella was unwilling to share her dream of becoming a children's author/illustrator with just anyone. She had made a habit of protecting her ideas from anyone who might squelch her creativity. She suspected someone as business oriented as Hawk just might be inclined to laugh at her modest dreams.

He surprised her, however, by saying, "It's a charming hobby. One I wouldn't mind cultivating myself. It looks like it might come in mighty handy at bedtime."

Ella smiled. Bedtime was clearly a sore subject. For the past several nights she had heard Hawk struggling to get the children into bed and keep them there. Figuring her shift was over once her pajamas were on, she allowed Hawk and herself the dignity of managing the children in his own loving, though admittedly inept, fashion. Both children asked to stay up later than what Hawk had decreed as bedtime, requested glasses of water and then, of course, extra trips to the bathroom, and generally did everything in their power to play their father like a Stradivarius. Just about the time Ella would mentally declare Hawk to be unsuited for fatherhood, she would hear the sound of Dr. Seuss stories floating down the hallway and be carried away to happier memories of her own. Hawk's readings were followed by the same nighttime prayer she had uttered when her mother was still around to tuck her in. Ella knew any father was better than one who ran away from his responsibilities like her old man had. Hawk was trying, God bless his heart. As far as she was concerned that in itself held redemption.

Ella couldn't help but wish there was somebody in her life who wanted to tuck her in. Someone with a sensuous voice, eyes as fathomless as a deep wishing well, and a heart more tender than one might first suspect.

Five

Wednesday nights soon became a weekly ordeal, the nature of which was akin to school assemblies that everyone knew they *should* appreciate but secretly dreaded. Wednesday was the day Ella left her charges in their father's sole care to drive into town for her art class.

Since Ella's desire for this class had been stated right up front and because Hawk didn't want to deny anyone the opportunity to explore their talents, he bid the children to put on a cheerful face as they saw their nanny off on her first excursion without them.

It was hard not to feel just a little hurt by the excitement in her face at the prospect of taking time away from them. She seemed to glow with the prospect of spending the evening with interesting people of her own age. This served to make Hawk feel older than his years. Long past the time it was still actually visible, Billy and Sarah watched the puff of dust that followed Ella's vehicle down the long dirt road that led into their paved driveway.

Hawk tried approaching the evening as an opportunity to grow closer to his children without having to compete with Ella's wonderful imagination and genuine childlike focus. He was determined to show Billy and Sarah that he could be just as much fun as a virtual stranger he'd hired off the street. Seeing no reason why a business-type agenda couldn't be applied to a family night, he carefully mapped out a series of meaningful and educational activities to fill their time most productively. He broached the subject with a bright smile.

"I bought you some new games."

"What kind of games?" they asked skeptically.

"Fun ones," he replied grimly.

Donning the look of martyrs, Billy and Sarah filed dutifully into the house, passing the television set with open longing upon their faces.

"Can we just watch cartoons instead?" Billy suggested.

"No."

The word came out flat and irrevocable. It mattered little to Hawk that Ella had restricted their TV time so that they might actually appreciate the opportunity to watch their big screen. All his heart heard was that his children would rather affix themselves to the TV than to him. The first game of the evening was set up with all the determination of a patriarchal gladiator.

"Trust me, this is going to be great, educational fun," he assured them.

Unfortunately, Hawk was the one who got the best education. He quickly discovered that the game he had purchased was designed more for yuppie parents than for their children. Nonetheless, he tried to remain positive.

Having covertly observed Ella's interactions with his children, he attempted to mimic some of her more effective techniques.

"But Ella doesn't do it that way," Sarah told her father for the umpteenth time at another of his suggestions for making the evening more pleasant.

"I don't care how Ella does it," he exploded. "This is the way I do things!"

Soon what started out as a way to facilitate closeness among family members began to feel like punishment. When Hawk overcooked the microwave popcorn, the stench was so overwhelming that everyone, including himself, lost their taste for it. After hearing Sarah and Billy repeatedly complain that "this was stupid," Hawk slammed the board game shut and threw it in the trash. Had his children been his employees, he would have simply fired them.

As it was, he felt like handing them his resignation.

Marching over to the television set in defeat, he remembered how much easier his life had been when he had simply compartmentalized it into separate work and home boxes. Indeed, the male provider mentality that had driven so much of his life was far less stressful than managing a home and two willful children alone. Up until his wife's untimely death, being a good provider was all Hawk knew about parenting. Fate certainly had a way of making people reassess their lives. Especially those built upon lies.

Grabbing a financial magazine off the end table, Hawk awaited Ella's return with a mixture of resentment and anticipation.

Three hours later Ella was asking, "Why is the TV so loud?"

Assaulted by the volume the instant she opened the front door, what she really wanted to know was why the blasted thing was on at all. Hadn't her presence and preference for creative activities made any impact on this family at all?

No one answered her question. She tiptoed over to the couch where the sleeping forms of the children were huddled beneath afghans that their grandmother had made for them. Hawk, too, had apparently fallen asleep watching cartoons. In the semidarkness of a room illuminated only by the eerie glow of the television set, he looked like a fallen warrior.

Ella's breath caught in her throat at the sight. She longed to touch his dark hair where it curled at his neckline and see if the texture was as soft as she remembered. Reminded of the story of Sleeping Beauty, she wondered if a stolen kiss would go unnoticed or, since gender roles were reversed, whether a princess even had the power to awaken a dreaming prince. The thought sent a quiver all the way through her body.

Storing the idea away as a potential story idea, Ella drew the afghan that had slipped around Hawk's waist to cover his arms. Wearing only a T-shirt and jeans, he was incredibly good-looking. His feet were bare as were the arms folded across his chest. Even slumber could not disguise the muscles corded beneath his forearms. She had heard him working out once or twice in the exercise room that she had initially assumed was just for show. He certainly put that pimply, young model from her art class to shame.

How Ella longed to paint Hawk exactly in this pose. In sleep, his chiseled features lost all haughtiness. The day's worth of stubble that shadowed his lower jaw and upper lip combined with the T-shirt stretched taut over his chest gave him a certain James Dean bad boy allure that coaxed a sigh from his appreciative audience. Indeed, he was the most gorgeous specimen of manhood Ella had ever dared to inspect so up close and personal.

Since lusting after him while he was sleeping seemed somehow immoral, she determined to put her wayward thoughts to bed along with this man's two adorable children. She reached for the remote control which was wedged between the chair cushions. Without warning, a hand reached out to encircle her wrist. Ella gasped.

How long had he been awake?

"I didn't mean to scare you," Hawk told her gently.

That deep voice coming out of the darkness was as captivating as his touch. She entertained a vision of him pulling her into his lap and smothering her with more of those mind-drugging kisses with which he parted so sparingly.

"Let me go," she said huskily.

He did, and the act left her feeling bereft. To cover the knocking of her foolish heart, she pointed the remote at him like a phaser off an old science fiction movie.

"Do you mind if I turn it down?" she asked, not waiting for his permission to mute the sound.

"You can shut it off for all I care," Hawk replied.

The look on his face dared her to criticize his use of an electronic baby-sitter in her absence. Although he dearly wanted to know exactly why Ella was home so late, he didn't ask. What this young woman did with her one night off a week was, after all, none of his business.

"How was class?" he asked offhandedly.

The look of joy that flitted across Ella's pretty features was unmistakable.

"It was wonderful, actually," she admitted, recalling the rare compliment the instructor had paid her in front of the rest of the class. Mr. Jenkins seemed to think that she had real talent—something seldom uttered aloud in college courses for fear that it might somehow corrupt one's artistic soul. To Ella his kind words were like droplets of rain upon a wilting blossom. Over her lifetime, she had endured far more barbs than compliments. So much so, in fact, that she tended to be suspicious whenever any praise came her way.

Hawk wanted to look deeper into that rapturous answer she had given. Was it wonderful because she was infatuated with her instructor? Or because some young college swain had turned her head? Or just because she was glad to be away from Fort Bedlam for the evening?

Hawk wondered how long had it been since anything had given him as much pleasure as art class gave this lovely ingenue. Lately it seemed his business owned him rather than the other way around. He couldn't remember the last time he had taken any sort of excursion other than to the bathroom in the middle of the night with a child who'd had an extra glass of water before falling asleep. Was it any wonder that he was out of touch with the concept of having fun?

The sight of Ella struggling to pick Sarah up off the couch all wrapped up in an afghan caused something rusty to twist in Hawk's chest.

"Let me do that," he told her, taking his sleeping angel girl from her arms.

"I'll turn her covers back," Ella said quietly so as not to awaken her.

In the soft glow of the television tube, Hawk looked sexier than any man had a right to after a night of baby-sitting. His hair was mussed and the top snap of his jeans undone. It was all Ella could do to keep her eyes from drifting down in an inappropriate direction. The sight of him holding a child in his arms didn't make Ella's heart beat any slower. In fact, that display of paternal instinct deepened the attraction she'd been fighting from the moment she first laid eyes on this man.

Hawk placed a tender kiss upon his daughter's forehead before turning out the light and heading back to the living room for his son. Ella wished she could sleep as soundly as the two children whom they transferred to their respective beds without so much as a peep from either of them. Tucking a favorite stuffed animal into bed with each one, she murmured "Sweet dreams" to them. Knowing that Billy was afraid of the dark, she stopped to make sure his night-light was on.

Oh, that it were so easy to dispel the monsters that followed one into adulthood!

A silent sentry, Hawk stood over his son's bed for a long while. Feeling like he had failed both his children in the past, he intended to protect them against any evil the world might have in store for them.

"He's beautiful," Ella whispered, brushing aside a lock of Billy's black hair from his forehead. "Both of your children are beautiful—inside and out."

As are you, Hawk thought to himself. Irritated with himself for almost speaking the words aloud, he reminded himself of his promise to keep his hands and his errant thoughts to himself. Just one night holding the fort down by himself was a powerful reminder of how hopeless he was without Ella's help. Having struck an agreement with her just the other morning over burned bacon, he could ill afford to scare her away with his libidinous thoughts.

Deliberately Hawk searched for safe ground. "If I haven't told you yet, I think you're terrific with them," he told her sincerely. "I want to thank you for everything you do—for all of us."

The compliment warmed Ella from the inside out. The heat it generated was reflected in the gentle smile that she bestowed upon him.

"You're welcome," she said, not trusting her heart to say more. Over the years, she could count on one hand the number of people who had offered such genuine appreciation of her talents. "They're really wonderful company."

Hawk's lips curved into a lopsided grin. Having just spent the night wrestling with them on what felt like every single insignificant issue from popcorn to Popeye, he was physically and emotionally bushed.

"You're too modest."

He was on the verge of telling her that if her artistic talents were equal to her child-rearing skills, he had no doubt she would go far. Just then Billy flung an arm across his pillow and cried out in his sleep.

Ella heard the word as clearly as if it had been a gunshot.

"Mommy!"

Hawk looked so stricken by that single word that it stopped Ella from bending down and comforting the child as instinct would have her do naturally. She didn't need reminding that she was the interloper here. Perhaps Hawk was frightened that Billy would awake and in his confusion mistake her for his mother. No one needed to tell Ella just how disastrous that could be. Already she worried that the children were projecting their need for a mother upon her. When the time came that she had to leave them for more than just a Wednesday night class, she didn't want to be responsible for crushing their tender feelings. One day she must leave for good, and she couldn't afford to leave her poor, battered heart behind, either.

"Shh...." Hawk crooned, bending down and cuddling the quivering boy in his arms. "It's me, Billy, your daddy. Everything's fine. You're dreaming again."

Billy's eyes fluttered open. Ella stepped back into the shadows and dabbed at her own eyes with the back of her hand. It grieved her to see this little boy hurting so. How many times in the orphanage had she cried out in her sleep for her mother only to have the night orderly tell her to "shut up and go back to sleep"?

The sight of Billy clinging to his father's neck made her want to weep. Maybe Hawk didn't know how to play with his children on their level. Maybe he vacillated between being too gruff with them one moment and too indulgent the next. But despite his failings, this man was light-years ahead of her father in the parenting department. He hadn't run out on his children when times got tough. Or sent them away to some fancy boarding school where money assuaged more than one wealthy parent's conscience. Hawk was here trying his best to keep his family and himself from falling apart.

Clearly he missed his beautiful wife as much as his children missed their mother. Other than in her dreams, Ella couldn't imagine being loved so completely. She knew only that being the center of a family that adored you would have to be the most wonderful, fulfilling feeling in the world. Lauren's life had been so tragically cut short, yet in some ways she had been a very lucky woman indeed.

Watching Hawk rock his son gently in his arms made Ella feel like a voyeur. Like someone separated from real life by a thick plate glass window. Her arms ached with emptiness as she silently backed out of the room and allowed Hawk the privacy he needed to heal two broken hearts in his own courageous way.

Six

Hawk looked tired the next morning as he dragged himself to the breakfast table. For the first few months after his wife's death, the children had both regularly cried out in their sleep for their mother. Since Ella had moved in, Hawk had taken the fact that these disturbing episodes had tapered off as a positive sign that the children were letting go of their grief and moving on with their lives.

The incident last night with Billy had evoked in Hawk such mixed feelings that he had sat up for hours afterward trying to sort them out. He didn't know whatever possessed him to think he could juggle all the responsibilities of mother, father and sole provider for his children *and* do justice to a company that employed numerous people who counted on him to continue making outrageous profits from afar.

Thank God for Ella. Hawk took comfort in watching her bustle around the kitchen with a song on her lips. Who was he kidding? It wasn't he who was providing the stability in his children's lives that they so desperately needed, but rather this lovely creature who had somehow found the time among all her other duties to master the expensive espresso machine Hawk had never once used since it had been out of the box.

The strong, sweet flavor of the coffee was a pleasant eye-opener after such a restless night. He appreciated Ella's sensitivity in allowing him time alone with his son and their shared memories. The look of pity he had spied in her eyes before she had quietly excused herself last night had been almost more than Hawk could bear. He'd had his fair share of pity surrounding Lauren's death. If the truth were known, that alone was partially responsible for his moving to Wyoming where so few people were privy to his past.

Hawk spread the morning newspaper on the kitchen table and proceeded to take solace in the financial pages. He mumbled a thank-you to Ella for preparing breakfast and immersed himself in the latest stock quotes.

Personally, she found his preoccupation with business as boring as cold oatmeal, which she was tempted to serve tomorrow morning for all the attention he paid her western omelette. Ella glanced outside and established that the day was bound to prove difficult. The wind had gusted up and was splattering raindrops against the bay window. Knowing it would be challenging keeping the children quietly occupied inside while their father attended to business, she racked her brain to come up with several suitable activities.

After clearing the table, she resorted to her faithful ironing board for story time. The children were still wearing their pajamas as she had eventually succumbed to Billy's logic that there wasn't any point in getting dressed if they couldn't go outside. Picking up one of Hawk's expensive Italian shirts and placing it on the end of the board, Ella proceeded to tell them the Indian legend of the Dream Catcher. It was a story of a brave boy plagued by nightmares that left him quivering like an aspen leaf beset by the winds of change. This particular Indian brave set forth on a journey quest to find just the right talisman to protect him in his sleep when a bow and arrow proved so useless. This he wove into a shield which he placed above his teepee door. Thenceforth only happy memories and sweet dreams were allowed through this magical weaving. Nightmares were caught like flies upon a spider's web and denied entrance.

"Do you know where we could buy a dream catcher?" Billy asked, his eyes widening at the prospect.

"No, but I'd be glad to show you how to make your own," she told him.

Agreeing that this was a very fine idea indeed, the children both scurried off to transfer Ella's magic bag from her bedroom to the rec room. It was nothing more than an old gunnysack filled with art supplies and bits of cloth and yarn. She showed them how to macramé their own unique dream catchers and how to attach their own special charms to give them mystical powers. Sarah chose seashells she had picked up on the beach with her grandparents and a "jewel" from her treasure box that Aunt Frannie on her mother's side had given her. Billy fashioned to his dream catcher a golden locket with a picture of his mother nestled inside. Ella picked a feather to symbolize her freedom, a dried Indian paintbrush blossom for creativity and a gaudy plastic ring from a Cracker Jack popcorn box for hope.

By noon, their dream catchers were done and hanging above their respective beds. The rain showed no sign of slackening. Hawk took a break from work only long enough to look surprised by the lunch his children served him. They greeted him with horribly affected French accents and dish towels draped over their arms.

"Welcome to Mountain View Bistro," they told him, seating him at the dining table with a flourish.

Hawk looked at the meal they set before him askance. He was grateful when Sarah presented him with a menu. Shaky lettering written in crayon proudly announced "Pigs in Blankets" as the main entrée. This proved to be hot dogs rolled up in crescent dough. A "Relish Kabob" was an orange skewered with toothpicks brandishing carrot strips and celery bits. The pièce de résistance was a "Sparkling Soda" that consisted of grape pop with two scoops of vanilla ice cream floating atop. It reminded Hawk of the Titanic just before it sank.

Smiling brightly, he praised them for their considerable efforts. They stood beside him eagerly awaiting his every bite. There was no chance whatsoever that they would leave his side long enough for him to scrape his plate into the trash can and pretend it had all been delicious. Touched that they had gone to such trouble for him, he moaned in pleasure with every bite he took.

"Umm," he mumbled, washing down his crispy hot dog with a slurp of purple glop. "Good. Very good." He swallowed. "Excellent, in fact."

Two sticky kisses on both cheeks made his sacrifice worthwhile. Still certain that he heard Ella giggling uncontrollably in the kitchen, he vowed to get even with her later.

The children grew restless as the inclement weather continued throughout the day. Not used to being cooped up for so long without benefit of television or video games, they began whining. Ella assured them that she knew the perfect rainy day activity to tide them over until their scheduled midday nap. She set out several sheets of slick art paper on the tiled section of the rec room floor and told them to roll up their pajama sleeves. Following her lead, they discovered the joys of finger painting. Squealing in delight at the feel of cool, bright colors squishing between their fingers, they began creating an array of original artwork.

Ella enjoyed the activity very much herself, forming a benevolent sun face out of swirls of red, orange and yellow. While she would have been the first to admit that finger painting was not a particularly quiet activity, it elicited in her another idea for a children's story.

It evoked something else entirely in Hawk. He stormed into the rec room with a portable phone in one hand and a look of exasperation upon his face. Seeing the mess his children were making of themselves as well as his house, he blew up.

"I was trying to talk on the phone," he said in a curt tone of voice, "and I could barely hear over all the noise you're making."

Ella's first instinct was to apologize for getting on her boss's nerves. Over the years she'd said plenty of "I'm sorrys." Still, something about the stricken expressions on the children's faces made her stand her ground. This was their home as much as it was his, after all, and it was hardly fair to expect children to behave like little adults.

"Creativity isn't always quiet," she told Hawk in a matter of fact manner. "Nor is it as tidy as stock reports. Fun doesn't necessarily line up in neat, orderly little boxes on a computerized grid." Ella shook her full head of auburn curls at him. "Is it too much to expect a man like you to appreciate that?"

Hawk pointed the phone in his hand at her. "What a

man like me appreciates is a little peace and quiet in my own home while I'm trying to get some work done,'' he replied stiffly.

Billy's and Sarah's eyes grew wide at the confrontation. They had heard their mother and father argue several times before over something called a boarding school, but never had they witnessed firsthand two grownups fighting over the concept of fun. It seemed to parallel preschool squabbles over a box of crayons.

Aware of their impressionable little eyes riveted to him, Hawk told Ella, ''I'm going to put the children down for their nap. When I return, I'd like to have a word with you, Ms. McBride.''

Ella mimicked his formality by employing her best Myrna Lloyd impression. ''I think that's a splendid idea, Mr. Hawk the third. Just remember while you're tucking your children in that you agreed not to question my methods—however unconventional they might seem.''

Although Hawk took umbrage with her tone of voice, Ella's words did strike a chord in his memory. Of course he had agreed to her silly stipulation when he'd hired her, but he had been desperate at the time. He glared at her before marching the children to the bathroom and instructing them to wash up. They didn't give him any grief about taking their naps. A whole day of keeping up with Ella had them completely tuckered out. They were asleep before Hawk was able to close the door of the rec room and square up with the help. He mentally corrected himself. *The wreck room…*

Ella had the place relatively picked up by the time he returned, making him feel all the more foolish for causing such a fuss in the first place. The tile floor was perfect for the water-based finger paints she was sponging up on her hands and knees. The sight was so unexpectedly erotic that it stopped Hawk in midstride. He knew his anger had far less to do with the state of his home than it did with the state of his libido.

After the awful, albeit adorable, lunch to which he'd been subjected, Hawk discovered, much to his dismay, that he didn't want to go back to work. That, in itself, was a first for him. Known far and wide as a workaholic, he was the type of man who used work as a way of avoiding deep personal reflection. That the sound of his children and his nanny at play could so distract him would have come as a shock to Hawk's business rivals and cohorts. That he actually felt jealous of the young woman he had hired to watch over his children came as a shock to *him* as well.

"We need to talk," he said by way of introduction.

"About what?" Ella asked, unwittingly wiggling her trim backside in an attempt to get a dried-up splotch of paint off the tiling.

"About maintaining some semblance of order in my home," he began stiffly.

"Like before I got here?" she asked sweetly, hoping there would be no need to further remind him of the chaotic state of affairs she had discovered that fateful day his children had wandered off unsupervised.

"Like expecting my children to be out of their pajamas by—" he checked his watch "—say, three o'clock in the afternoon."

"Did you want me to dress them in formal attire for naptime?" Ella countered, pointing out the fact that they were in bed at the moment.

Realizing how hopeless it would be to try and keep her job if Hawk didn't approve of her methods, Ella decided to be frank. She put her sponge down and sat up on her haunches.

"Look," she said evenly. "I know that a logical, sequential business type such as yourself might have difficulty understanding someone like me."

She forgot to mention *uptight*, Hawk thought to himself, taking offense at her stereotypical assessment of him.

"And what type might you be?" he asked darkly.

"Creative and abstract, of course."

Hawk thought he must have fallen into one of those women magazine quizzes that always categorized stable men like himself as an unsuitable mate.

"Take a minute to look at this," Ella told him, holding up a sheet of artwork that was already beginning to curl at the edges. "Really look at it."

Hawk came closer to get a better look. He had no idea what it was supposed to be. Ella handed it to him.

"I think it shows amazing promise for a four-year-old. It's a pair of flying dragons," she explained, turning it right side up for him. The creatures were resplendent against a purple and blue sky.

Hawk smiled. "I know just the place for this."

Ella hoped he didn't mean the garbage can. "On the refrigerator?" she prompted.

"No. Over my computer."

"Over the screen, I hope you mean," she ventured under her breath.

Hawk squatted down beside her on the hard tile floor. "Is that so?" he asked. Picking up the soapy sponge, he offered his help.

Ella couldn't help admiring his marvelous forearms as Hawk demonstrated what effect muscles had upon a stained floor. The effect they had on Ella's senses was equally devastating.

"And what, pray tell, did you mean by that last mumbled comment?"

Having made a lifelong practice of traipsing merrily along where angels dared to tread, Ella considered her options in answering that particular inquiry. All she had to lose by being honest was the best job she had ever stumbled into.

"I'm sure you're a terrific CEO and all," she told her boss, turning eyes the color of spring meadows upon him. "It's just that sometimes I think you forget that your children aren't your employees."

"Are you forgetting that *you* are?" Hawk asked pointedly.

He asked the question only to remind himself that Ella's status should preclude the kind of wanton thoughts he was entertaining about her. He hadn't meant it to stiffen her spine against him.

She drew herself up. The low, deep tone of his voice and the intimacy of their proximity set her pulse skittering down the path of costly mistakes.

"Not for a minute," Ella told him with a smile born of unflinching candor. "All I'm trying to say is that I think you're doing a terrific job for a single father."

Hawk's eyes softened at the compliment. It wasn't at all what he expected. Nonetheless, he braced himself for the rest of her commentary.

"It's just that I think you could use a little help loosening the old corporate tie so to speak."

Hawk tugged at the open collar of his navy polo shirt. "Is that so?" he asked drolly.

Ella nodded her head, regretting at this point, ever venturing into such personal territory.

"And what if that proves dangerous, Ms. McBride?"

Ella wrinkled her head in confusion. "Dangerous?"

Hawk reached over to dip his index finger into an open container of paint and proceeded to transfer a drop to the tip of Ella's pert nose. The bright spot of red made her look like a clown. A very sexy clown.

"Like letting a tiger out of a cage," he told her by way of explanation. His voice was a predatory growl.

"Or opening Pandora's box?" she offered by way of extending the comparison.

Ella's green eyes widened in comprehension as she smeared a line of yellow paint across the bridge of Hawk's nose. A matching stripe of red made him look like a fearsome warrior.

Indeed his blood was running hot and fast as if he were in fact preparing for combat. He just didn't want Ella to be a casualty in the battle of the sexes. In the war he was waging inside himself.

Catching her by the wrist as she drew her arm away, he told her solemnly, "Playing with me could get rough. You might want to think about running away while I'm still inclined to let you."

The memory of his kisses was enough to keep her rooted to the spot. "I'm a big girl," she assured him in a throaty whisper.

She ran her free hand up the length of Hawk's arm, smearing it with paint. The feel of that cool pigment on his skin stirred in him manly urges too long suppressed. The desire mirrored in Ella's eyes was all the permission he needed.

Hawk reached for the top button of her paint-spackled white cotton shirt. The button pulled free, and he dabbed a spot of yellow at the base of her creamy throat. Ella's pulse throbbed beneath the signature he left on her skin.

"You're sure?" he asked, giving her one final chance to save herself.

"Positive," she assured him.

Cupping his proud jaw into both her hands, Ella kissed

him soundly. His lips were warm and firm. His tongue hungry. Scorched by the heat of his all-consuming need, she pulled away. Rather than seeking composure, she tossed her glorious mane of hair back and reveled in the sensation of being devoured alive by the blue flame of desire.

Hawk reached for the next button but found he hadn't the patience to undo them one by one. Instead he ripped the front of her blouse open, popping the entire row of buttons off like so many snaps. Beneath that baggy, utilitarian shirt was a lacy bra molded to the most perfect breasts Hawk had ever seen. Ella was breathing hard, causing the swell of those breasts to rise and fall in the most erotic manner.

Worried that he would find her too unfashionably well-developed, Ella fought against the urge to cover herself from the harsh glare of the lights overhead. That Hawk paid her homage with her name on his lips made her feel lovelier than she had ever thought possible. Dipping his hand into the paint once again, he traced the curve of her breasts with his fingertips. Ella quivered beneath his touch. Kneeling beside her, Hawk bent down and suckled each hard nipple through the lacy fabric that held her captive.

Ella moaned when he pronounced her beautiful. She knew better than to trust any flattery uttered in the heat of passion. Still the compliment warmed her heart. She was no shy virgin, but up until now her experience had been limited and relatively awkward. This was as close to heaven as she had ever come. Cradling his head between her breasts, she gasped in pleasure when he took the clasp of her bra between his teeth and nipped it open.

Ella toppled over backward on the floor, pulling him over with her. Paint splattered everywhere. Hawk raised himself from her prone body to worship at its altar. This, he thought over the pounding in his head, was the way God intended a woman's body to look, and to feel. Rounded, voluptuous, welcoming. Dipping his fingers in the paint, he trailed them over the curve of her breasts, down the hollow beneath her rib cage, to stop at the snap of her jeans.

"I apologize," she told him with a wobbly smile intended to give him consent to push the envelope even further. "It seems you have a great deal to teach me about having fun after all."

"I make you no promises," Hawk told her softly.

In no mood for a discussion, Ella reached down and undid her jeans herself. "Would it help to know that I'm not looking for a long-term bond—just an unguarded heart?"

That in itself was asking a great deal from a man whose heart was fortified behind mighty castle walls. Ella squiggled out of her jeans and skimpy panties. Realizing that she lay naked with a fully clothed man kneeling between her legs, she reached for his shirt. Hawk was more than willing to assist her in divesting himself of it. He shrugged off his slacks and socks in no time as well, kicking them out of the way. Ella yanked his briefs down about his ankles and rolled him onto his back.

"My turn," she purred in a voice so throaty that she almost didn't recognize it as belonging to herself.

Using Hawk's chest as a canvas, Ella mixed the colors of the rainbow into a mat of dark hair. A Greek sculpture in flesh and blood, his body was a glorious tribute to mortal beauty. Ella paid it tribute with her eyes and her hands. Splaying them across his heart, she painted in lustful strokes that had him moaning for release. It had been a long time since Hawk had made love, well before Lauren's death, if the truth were known, and *never* in such a bold, untempered fashion.

Dragging her down to his lips, Hawk kissed her over and over again, indulging in the feel of their paint-smeared bodies sliding against one another. Positioning her beneath him, he discovered it was hard restraining this woman to one place. They started on the tile, but by the time Hawk parted her legs with his knees, they had somehow made their way onto the carpet. Mindless of rug burns, they writhed on the floor, joining body and soul.

Ella gasped as he entered her. He had looked enormous in his aroused state. So big in fact that she feared he would hurt her if he didn't take care not to. She was so wet and ready, however, that her fears proved unfounded. The pleasure he rendered overshadowed any lingering soreness that would surely remind her later that she had been thoroughly loved. Neither of them paid any attention to the end table they overturned in the midst of their passion. A lamp and some pictures went crashing to the floor.

It was all Ella could do to keep from screaming every time Hawk took her to the edge of ecstasy and back again. She read the gratification in his face each time he felt her climax, taking his own pleasure to a higher plateau. Shuddering, he poured himself in her, calling out her name as if it were a prayer upon his lips. Feeling more joy than she thought a single woman was entitled to, Ella gave him safe refuge in her arms and her heart. Spent and satiated they lay there a long while.

Paint was everywhere. In their hair. Between their thighs. On the floor and walls. Even a speck or two on the ceiling. Though he had been the one to complain initially about the mess, Hawk wasn't concerned in the least.

"I'll start the shower," he told Ella. "Join me."

Hissy Face took this opportunity to dash out from beneath the couch and race across the floor. Multicolored paw prints marked her path. Ella picked up her ruined shirt and held it in front of her. For the first time since their passion had flared, she gave thought to the children. What would they think if they were to walk into this disaster area while both she and their father were standing there buck-naked?

"Just a minute," she told him, stopping to slip into her shirt and straighten an overturned lamp. On the floor beside it lay a picture. Lauren's gorgeous face stared accusingly at her from behind broken glass.

Ella felt a pang of guilt.

And resentment.

How was someone as plain and unsophisticated as she supposed to compete with such golden perfection, with a ghost who had just watched her making passionate love with her husband?

"Shut up," Ella told the woman, turning her face down.

With that, she left to join Hawk in the act of washing away all signs of their flagrant indiscretion.

Seven

Cleaning up was almost as much fun as getting dirty. After tiptoeing upstairs to check on the still-napping children, Ella slipped into the shower with Hawk. He liked it hot. Languid heated showers were but another luxury Ella had yet to grow used to. They had decided advantages over bathing in the creek as she was accustomed to doing. Lathering her hands up with expensive, fragrant soap, she proceeded to wash the paint off all the places Hawk couldn't reach by himself.

"You wash my back, and I'll wash yours," he suggested in a tone that matched the water's temperature.

Ella willingly obliged, running soapy palms across the expanse of Hawk's broad, muscled back. Satisfied that she had done an adequate job there, she slid her hands under his arms and cuddled up against him. His pectoral muscles felt hard and well defined beneath a mat of dark chest hair. Spooning her body against his backside, Ella was pleased to hear him sigh in contentment at the weight of her breasts and the soft feel of her downy mons as she slid across his back.

The hot water soothed away the soreness in Ella's muscles and between her thighs. Hawk's ministering touch was even more healing. They shampooed each other thoroughly, washing all traces of body art down the drain. His preoccupation with sudsing up her breasts made her grateful for once in her life for her rather generous endowment. All her life she had wished for a lithe, society-thin figure like Lauren's as displayed in photos littering the mantelpiece. Many times Ella had cursed the middle button pulling on any given shirt. Suddenly that middle button lost its ability to make her grit her teeth in frustration.

She was gritting her teeth now, but for an entirely different reason. One that had her grabbing the showerhead to steady herself as Hawk played with her nipples, intent on making them expand beneath his patient ministration. It seemed he was intent on bringing her to yet another orgasm before allowing her out of the shower.

Not one to turn away such an exquisite indulgence when it was offered, Ella yielded, sinking a few moments later to the floor of the huge tub in an exhausted heap. The water beat down upon her in a lukewarm cascade. It seemed the water heater was giving out at last. Hawk turned off the faucet and pulled her into his arms.

"You are the most phenomenal woman I have ever encountered in all my life," he told her.

Those words almost knocked Ella off her feet again. Clinging to his neck for support, she whispered in his ear, "That's only because I succumbed to your charms so easily, you wicked man."

Hawk laughed. Ella hoped he hadn't mentally shortened her comment to mean only that she was easy.

Nothing could be further from the truth. Her sexual experiences had been few and far between. Her first serious crush, a nineteen-year-old drummer who paid Ella the first real romantic attention she'd ever received, taught her that sex did not automatically equate to love. She vowed to be more discerning when the band pulled out of town leaving her feeling cheap and used. Her last exploit had been with a great tipper who had gallantly defended her honor when another customer had surreptitiously pinched her bottom causing her to drop her entire order on the floor. Ella discovered later that her valiant knight had a wife and two kids waiting for him back in Seattle. The creep actually deemed it a consolation to offer to put her on his permanent sales route through the area.

Stepping into the comfort of the biggest, softest, whitest towel she had ever seen, Ella prayed that her pattern of self-destructive relationships was about to take a turn for the better. Opening the bathroom door, she saw Sarah just turning the corner down the hallway. Though a talented storyteller, Ella had no desire to explain her reasons for emerging from Hawk's bathroom wearing nothing more than a towel to his baby girl with anything other than the truth.

"If you'll wait for me in the kitchen, Sarah," she called after her, "I'll be there in a minute to fix you a snack."

"Okay," the girl called back, apparently satisfied that all was right with the world.

Ella wished it were so easy to put things right for Hawk. Though initially touched to discover he had cleaned up the mess in the rec room leaving absolutely no trace of their passionate lovemaking behind, it later occurred to Ella that in doing so Hawk was actually trying to erase the incident from his mind as well. He hid behind the computer for the rest of the day and at dinner seemed to have a hard time making direct eye contact with her. Afterward, he retreated to the den to read the newspaper and didn't offer to join in their evening games as he had the night before. Faking a yawn, he went to bed earlier than usual, for the first time ever leaving Ella to tuck the children in herself.

Ella checked her heart for injuries. Though substantial, she hoped to survive the romantic tremors shaking her faith in her ability to ever find an emotionally satisfying relationship. Still, it was gut wrenching to discover that what to her had been the most glorious moment of her life was an embarrassment to Hawk! When would she get it through her head that men preferred women who played hard to get? When Billy suggested "Old Maid" after dinner, Ella couldn't help feeling that it was destiny giving her another sign.

Hawk may as well have been reading the newspaper upside down for all the good it did him to try and concentrate on the business article he had started reading at least three times. Distracted by the sound of Ella and the children giggling over a game of cards, he found himself reevaluating not the stock market, but the choices he had made over the course of his lifetime. He had much to show in material gain for all his dedication and sacrifice. Still, money hadn't been the answer for Lauren who had put so much stock in it that she married "beneath" her just to ensure its continual flow in her life. Unlike her father, who had prestige but a dwindling fortune, Hawk lacked a pedigree but possessed a knack for making money.

If, however, Lauren's mistake had been marrying below her blue blood lines, Hawk's had been in marrying into high society in an attempt to buy the kind of prestige denied those of blue-collar backgrounds. Unfortunately, Hawk's new money never did smell quite as good to Lauren's jet set friends as did the shrinking piles of old money moldering away in the hands of a younger generation more into squandering than generating assets.

Listening to the fun his children were having in the next room, Hawk couldn't help but wonder if he wouldn't have been far happier had he decided to build a life with someone less assuming, less demanding and less concerned with what the world thought of them. Someone like Ella. Hawk wanted to attribute her refreshing attitude to her age. Having survived a less than perfect marriage, he wasn't eager to step into another any time soon. The mere thought of raising any more than his own two children left him with the cold sweats.

Just because he had experienced the warmest, most passionate sex of his life earlier in the day was no reason to go off half-cocked and start daydreaming about actually marrying that unconventional young woman in the other room. Hawk knew what a terrible disservice that would be to her. Such a charming, young creature had no business being fettered to a man as jaded as himself. In his early thirties, Hawk was far from being over the hill. Still, the decade separating his and Ella's ages seemed insurmountable to a man struggling to get his complicated life together. Knowing Ella, she would probably want a whole brood of children to raise. He doubted whether she could ever be tied down long to someone as pedestrian as he seemed in her presence. Lauren certainly hadn't.

Hawk already felt a twinge of possession seeping into his soul whenever Ella was near, and it frightened him. Abandoning his unread newspaper, he headed back to the shower. This time he intended to bathe alone—in cold,

cold water, in hopes it would banish all thoughts of the sensual creature who had awakened his carnal appetite with such a vengeance.

Hawk awoke earlier than usual to the sound of Ella's off-key humming outside his bedroom window. She was scattering seeds and stale bits of bread to the birds, who upon discovering her generosity, had begun congregating daily on the redwood deck. He knew just how they felt. He, too, wanted to be as near this beautiful, blithe spirit as trust would allow him. True to his name, Hawk kept his own wing tips poised toward fleet escape if his freedom were challenged.

Still in all, there were no signs of cages or captivity about Ella McBride as she settled into a soft-cushioned lawn chair with a sketch pad in hand. She looked lovely sitting there in the early morning light, savoring a cup of coffee before her long day of duties began. Previously unaware of his nanny's morning meditative practices, he vowed to set his alarm earlier in the future if it meant awakening to such quiet gracefulness. He pulled on a pair of jeans and a T-shirt, deciding to postpone his shower until after breakfast so that he could share a private moment with Ella before the children arose.

One moment she was sketching the sun caught in the branches of an apple tree and the next her light was blocked by a Greek god standing before her. Hawk took her breath away. He was just as sexy with a trace of stubble upon his jaw line as without. Though both looks suited him well, this tousled bad boy air turned Ella to mush. She had always been a sucker for a man who looked like he rode his Harley-Davidson motorcycle over bumpy roads.

"Mind if I join you?" Hawk asked, his voice a deep, resonant timbre that sent the birds seeking safety in the nearby trees.

Ella wished she had enough sense to join in their flight.

"Be my guest," she replied, setting her sketch down and giving him her full attention.

Avariciously eyeing her cup of coffee, Hawk cleared his throat. Twice. Clearly he was as nervous as she was about initiating conversation after the mind-boggling sex they had shared the day before. It didn't help matters any that she was wearing nothing more than an oversize night-shirt. Ella was mistaken if she thought it boring attire. Indeed, Hawk found it sexier than any of the exorbitantly priced Paris lingerie of which his wife had been so fond to the tune of literally thousands of dollars.

"We need to talk," he said at last, hypnotizing her with those soft gray eyes.

"Think so?"

Still hurt over the way he had emotionally ditched her after their mutual shower, she wasn't about to make this easy on him. All night long she had tossed and turned, working this predicament over in her mind looking for the vein of gold running through a discarded pebble. Having abandoned any pretense of being immune to Hawk, she knew it was totally useless wishing that she hadn't succumbed to her baser instincts. Ella supposed this was where she got her walking papers. And just as she suspected it was already too late to leave with her heart intact. Sarah and Billy had taken up permanent residence there. As well as their sexy daddy. Damn him all to pieces.

"Yes, I do," Hawk replied.

He was so startled by her feigned indifference that he almost wondered if he hadn't dreamed what had happened between them. His body certainly wouldn't let him get by with such a lame pretense. Already he was reacting to this woman with all the ardor of a man who remembered every womanly curve of her body pressed against his. He grew hard with the memory.

"Do I need to apologize?" he asked, fighting off the urge to rip off her clothes and reenact yesterday's rapture on the smooth redwood planking beneath them or the hot tub simmering beneath its cover on the deck next to them or anywhere on God's good earth that she would grant him access to her delectable body.

"I hope not," Ella replied stiffly, preparing herself for the old *it's not you, it's me* routine.

"I shouldn't have taken advantage of you like that," Hawk continued. Wanting to make sure she understood he held her blameless, his eyes never left hers. "You're young and susceptible, and it was wrong of me."

Ella smiled at his chivalrous attitude. "I'm not exactly Lolita, if that's what you're getting at," she told him evenly. "And you're not some celebrity grandpa looking for arm candy—as if anyone could ever mistake me for that—in a futile attempt to recapture his youth."

Ella refused to let the stunned expression on Hawk's face stop her from saying what was on her mind. Just because she would probably lose her job for what she was about to say didn't mean she was going to let this man labor under any false assumptions about her. If there was anything she despised, it was people presuming she was less than capable because of her age.

"I'm a very mature twenty-one, and I've been taking care of myself for a whole lot longer than this state's juvenile system would ever admit to in a court of law. So if you're laboring under the assumption that you took advantage of some silly college girl who expects a proposal from you, nothing could be further from the truth. I know you're on the rebound from your wife's death, and I respect your feelings for her. I also won't deny that I enjoyed every minute of what happened between us. Thoroughly, if you want to know the truth, and I'd do it again if given half the chance. So if you're not too uptight to see where this relationship leads, I'd actually like to give it a try. My guess is we're not particularly well suited, but I'm not ready to give up on you or your children just yet. Of course, I understand how I might make you uncomfortable, so if you still want to fire me, I'd like to remain friends,'' she said.

For a moment Hawk almost thought she was going to stick out her hand and ask him to shake on it. Where did this woman come up with such outlandish ideas? Ella's outspoken manner was a far cry from the kind of womanly wiles to which he'd been subjected in the past. Perhaps he had underestimated her part in what had led to their passionate encounter. He certainly had no intention of firing her. Not only would it go against his own sense of decency, his children would disown him.

''You are a most remarkable woman,'' he said, gathering his wits about him.

Certainly no one would ever accuse Ella McBride of pulling her punches. The power of her right hook presently had him on the ropes. So much so that he didn't bother countering her assumptions about how he felt about Lauren. It was such a painful subject for him that he refused to talk about it to anyone.

''Of course you still have a job for as long as you want one,'' he told her, avoiding more difficult subjects.

It almost bothered him that Ella didn't seem to consider herself beautiful as much as did her assumption that she deserved no better than a romp in the hay from him. Hawk took for granted that, presented with a similar tempting proposition to indulge in a sexually satisfying relationship without any strings attached, few of his male associates would think it sounded nearly as villainous as it did to him. Why, she might as well ask for extra for services rendered like some common prostitute instead of the precious gift she had bestowed upon him. Still, Ella was right about one thing. He was not ready to get down on bended knee and make the same mistake twice.

Whether he ever would have opened up to her about his distrust of the opposite sex, including a fear of gold diggers, not to mention his own insecurity about the way Lauren had misused him, was a moot point. Billy stepped out onto the deck rubbing his eyes and looking for breakfast. How very like the surrounding birds they all were in seeking Ella's comfort and support, Hawk thought to himself.

"You go ahead and finish your sketch," he told her. "I'll make breakfast today."

So touched by the offer that it almost brought tears to her eyes, Ella chided herself for being such a sap. It was, after all, the least Hawk could do when he had so politely brushed her off after the most incredible sex ever recorded. His refusal to talk about his late wife only confirmed what she already suspected. Theirs was a love that transcended time and space and even death. There was no way she could ever hope to compete with what he and Lauren had.

Although breakfast only proved to be cold cereal and milk with toast, Hawk's gesture was something dear to Ella. She poured herself a bowl of cereal and glanced outside.

It was a glorious day, the kind that begs to be spent outdoors amid sunshine and flowers and people. Ella was just about to toss Hawk's discarded newspaper in the trash when something caught her eye. She had forgotten that this was the weekend for the annual Frog Festival at Deer Valley, a small community nearby which consisted primarily of blue-collar workers employed at the local steel mill. By and large these hardworking people were convinced that education was the key to advancing their own children's chances at succeeding in life. Because the state of school finances left their buildings in deteriorating condition with no frills left over for maintaining extracurricular activities, the community came together once a year in a money-making project targeting a specific improvement project. This year they were working to refurbish the gym and hopefully have enough extra to buy a new scoreboard. After all, the Deer Valley Wranglers had come within a hair of winning the State Basketball Tournament the year before, and pride was high in the community.

For the past ten years the annual Frog Festival had become a favorite among locals and tourists alike. In the past Ella had volunteered her services at numerous booths. What fun it would be to partake of the festivities as a participant this year. When she asked the children if they would like to accompany her, they were wildly excited. They couldn't imagine what an official frog festival would have to offer, but after being cooped up all day yesterday because of the rain, they were certain to have a jolly time.

Hurt that no one thought to ask him along, Hawk decided to invite himself. That his children looked at him as if he had just sprouted an extra arm out of his forehead didn't dissuade him in the least. Sick and tired of spending every waking minute working, he was ready for a break. The thought of spending yet another day home alone with no one to converse with but electronic ''friends'' while

Ella and his children were off on another Mary Poppins adventure held little appeal for Hawk. Not to mention the fact that he was intrigued by Ella's suggestion that they give their strained relationship a chance to see where it might take them. That it was presently headed toward a frog festival came as no surprise to Hawk who had long ago come to the conclusion that any destination Ella chose was bound to be magical.

Eight

The Tenth Annual Frog Festival took place in the middle of Deer Valley City Park. The park was little more than an empty lot with a few well-used pieces of playground equipment scattered throughout. Still, it looked festive enough with brightly colored tents and homemade signs proudly proclaiming an array of booths. A schedule of events was posted at the entryway. For a dollar apiece adults were admitted to Lily Pad Land and directed to the nearest ticket booth. Children were let in free of charge.

After buying a fistful of tickets, Hawk followed Ella to the center tent where the highly anticipated and emotionally charged frog race was just about to begin. Participants placed bets on the amphibian of their choice and took their places outside a large circle drawn in the dirt with white paint. There they urged their respective frogs to be the first to jump outside the circle. Hawk placed a dozen tickets on Crazy Frog's Legs while Ella bet on Amphibious

Force. Sarah picked Polly Wog as a long shot, and Billy bet on Jeremiah the Bullfrog to win.

Polly Wog, the decided underfrog in the competition, edged out her closest competitor, Rana Pipiens, by a "nose" to win her backers an entire homemade boysenberry pie. The victors made their way to a nearby picnic table to enjoy their spoils. The pie was as delicious as the day itself. Nobody seemed to mind in the least that the children's mouths were stained bluish purple with berries by the end of the impromptu feast. Chock-full, they raced to the nearest set of swings, promising to come back the instant their father called them back to the table.

Ella stretched out on the bench and patted her full tummy. The clouds overhead revealed the faces of gods pleased to see mankind put aside their daily worries to indulge in a bit of fun. That it was all for a good cause made the pilgrimage that much more sanctioned in the heavens above. Dressed in nothing more than a pair of old cutoffs and a white T-shirt from a former Frog Festival appropriately covered with frogs in all manner of whimsical poses, Ella looked right at home. As she seemed to be wherever she was—whether that be driving Hawk's expensive car, under a benevolent sky, or beneath him. She looked lovely lying there with her glorious russet mane fanned about her face, innocently displaying her well-developed shape. Hawk thought the mountains had nothing on Ella's form.

Eager to try their skill at any number of surrounding booths, the children returned as promised without having to be summoned. As they wound their way through the open-air stalls, it seemed everyone knew Ella. Everywhere they turned someone was calling out her name. Hawk was duly impressed with her easy manner and her memory for names and faces—right up until a robust fellow sneaked up behind her and swung her right off her feet.

"Buzz!" she cried out in surprise.

Hawk thought it a fitting name for a man wearing a bullfrog hat that made him look utterly ridiculous—and young and fun and unfettered by the kind of worldly cares weighing down his own tired shoulders. As Ella introduced them, Hawk wondered if she had actually dated this young man in the past. However irrationally founded, Hawk felt threatened by the possibility.

"We need someone to fill in at the kissing booth," Buzz told Ella with a wink. He seemed to deliberately ignore Hawk's glaring presence. "And since I personally know the value of your kisses, I was hoping you wouldn't mind helping the cause."

Noting the playful punch Ella delivered to Buzz's shoulder, Hawk informed him coolly, "She most certainly does mind."

I mind very much, he mentally corrected himself. Ashamed of himself for speaking for her as if she weren't capable of making up her own mind, Hawk wondered what it was about Buzz's youthful exuberance and cocky attitude that made him want to drive his fist right through the fellow's smiling face.

As if reading his mind, or perhaps his menacing body language, Buzz leaned over to whisper in Ella's ear. "Why don't you lose the old guy and drop by the lake later in the day? We're having a keg, and a lot of your old friends from high school will be there. Phoebe's coming."

Hawk suspected that subtlety wasn't one of Buzz's strong suits. He couldn't help but think the younger man had intended his hushed tones to be overheard. Why Hawk found the thought of Ella attending a party with some of her old friends so disturbing was something he didn't want to discuss. Maybe it was selfish on his part, but he nonetheless held out fragile hope that she might actually prefer spending the evening supervising his children and spending time with him. Not likely, Hawk thought ruefully. It was unfair on his part to expect a beautiful, young woman to give up an evening socializing with people her own age for a chance at prolonging a dead-end relationship with him.

"I'll be over at the balloon catapult if you want to catch up with me later," Buzz added, raising his voice to a more courteous level. "It was nice to meet you, sir," he added as an afterthought to Hawk.

"Likewise," he replied dryly.

Hawk wasn't sure whether it was being called "sir," the reference to him being over the hill or the festive atmosphere that caused his more playful side to make a presence. Keeping Ella firmly rooted to his side, he browsed the booths with his children, indulging them in whatever they wanted: frog-shaped cookies, frog kites, frog hats and webbed footwear. Against his better judgment, he even bought them each a pet amphibian. No bigger than his thumb, the poor creatures were confined to jelly glasses with holes poked into the lids. Hawk swallowed nervously at the thought of what their playful kittens might do if they ever got hold of Billy's and Sarah's frogs. If the frogs were lucky, their proud new owners would yield to the urge to open their containers and unwittingly let their pets escape to the surrounding grass. At this very moment, children of all ages were combing the surrounding area for signs of frogs on the lam.

By the time they made their way over to the balloon catapult, Hawk had already proved his prowess by banging a sledgehammer onto a lever that sent a frog-faced marker upward past "tadpole powered," through the "average frogman range," and upward to "bullfrog heights" where a bell was ceremoniously rung to distinguish the accomplishment. As Hawk was collecting his prize, Buzz called Ella over to his booth. She good-naturedly gave him the price of five tickets for the privilege of letting him thoroughly soak her with oversize water balloons. When they switched roles, however, her projectiles fell far short of their mark leaving a grinning Buzz unscathed. Ella maintained that it was all in good fun, and Buzz thanked her profusely for promoting the booth. Indeed a crowd had gathered to watch the grownups' horseplay. Hawk was more inclined to think that little pervert Buzz had deliberately doused Ella in an attempt to host his own wet T-shirt contest. One in which Ella was bound to win. Hawk doubted whether she had any awareness at all of how incredibly beautiful she really was with her face shining and her shirt clinging to her voluptuous curves. That she thought herself less than stunning was typical of her total lack of self-awareness.

Hawk insisted on taking a turn at the catapult, positioning himself opposite of good old Buzz with an arsenal of hefty-size water balloons.

"Let me show you what an *old guy* can do," he said, launching his first attack.

His aim was flawless, drilling his hapless opponent right in the face. He hit his target three out of three tries and deftly sidestepped two out of three volleys himself. The children squealed in delight to see their father drench his adversary and actually get wet himself. Ella led the clapping as the dripping warriors bowed to their audience.

Looking in the direction of the "Froggie Goes a Courtin' Kissing Booth" Hawk saw that Buzz was right about the lack of interest displayed by all the eligible men available. The line had, in fact, dwindled to nothing. This was not particularly surprising considering the dour-faced maid positioned on the other side of the booth. One would think she would pay the customers instead of the other way around. Feeling guilty for such uncharitable thoughts, Hawk pulled Ella over to the booth and made a great show of dropping all his remaining tickets and a sizable bill into the receptacle placed there. He hoped Buzz was watching.

"Remember, this is for charity," Hawk said, taking her into his arms and crushing her with a movie screen kiss that left Ella holding on to him to keep from falling down.

Lack of privacy did not affect the potency of that all too public kiss, the thoroughness of which caused the earth to come to a complete stop and reverse the direction it was spinning. Ella's mind went numb. Public or private, she didn't think she could ever get enough of this man's kisses or the feel of his hard body pressed against hers. The fierce possessiveness that she saw reflected in his eyes filled her heart with hope.

Under the impression that it might well appear she was merely playing for the crowd, Ella kissed him back for all she was worth. Opening her mouth, she touched her tongue to his and darn near swooned right there in his arms. Recalling how hard she had worked to divest herself of the label, she hoped, dazedly, that Hawk hadn't actually been referring to her as a charity case when he pulled her into his embrace.

The crowd certainly didn't see it that way.

"Shucks," one of them called out. "It didn't work, princess—he's still a frog!"

"I'd pay a dollar for a kiss like that," declared another.

A woman, whom one could only assume was his wife, elbowed him sharply in the side. Ella laughed good-naturedly at their ribbing. Little did they know that she felt more frog herself than princess. It was far easier for her to cast Hawk as the knight in shining armor of whom she had dreamed as a girl. That he was out of her reach was a given. Nannies from across the way who lived in log cabins without running water or electricity were only asking for trouble if they aspired to change their rank through any means as fickle as love. Hard work and education were the only ways Ella knew to change her social position.

Shaking off those old, beloved fantasies that had helped her survive her difficult childhood was more difficult than Ella would have imagined. Naturally, looking at life realistically wasn't something reflected in her thinking or her artwork. She far preferred Don Quixote's outlook of viewing life as it should be, rather than as it was. Ella knew that a part of her would always cling to the fairy tales that her mother had read to her as an impressionable child, but she also reminded herself that right now it was enough to simply share some good times with Hawk and his precious children. Pinning her hopes on childhood dreams was simply asking to have her heart cut out.

Considering that their relationship was mutually beneficial, Ella saw no need to upset an already rocking boat. Hawk had offered her the financial security to pursue her education and ultimately her life's dream of becoming a "real" artist, not to mention the opportunity to be part of a real family—one that didn't treat her merely like a paid servant. For her part, Ella felt good about helping Hawk to become more spontaneous and less tied down by business concerns. Worried that he was heading for an early grave, she took it as a personal mission to help him discover what was truly most important in life before it was too late.

She had never undertaken a more rewarding mission in her life. It was, after all, a labor of love.

Love!

That fickle, double-edged word held Ella at bay. Having never known her father and losing her mother to cancer at such a young age, she came to associate love with loss early on in her life. That misconception was reinforced in a string of foster homes in which love was frequently only a word used to manipulate a vulnerable little girl trying her darnedest to ingratiate herself to those in control of her life. Looking back, Ella could honestly say that love hadn't gotten her anything more than a broken heart from her first crush, and her second, third and fourth for that matter.

As far back as she could remember, love was suspect.

Nonetheless it came knocking upon her heart asking for a place to stay. Though Ella doubted whether it would ever attempt to establish permanent residence, she didn't have the presence of mind to turn it away. Despite her determination to dismiss that foolish fantasy of someday falling in love with a wonderful man who would see past her freckles and red hair and come to cherish her for who she really was, Ella couldn't make herself let go of her lovely illusions. Walking around the Frog Festival on the arm of a real Prince Charming made it hard not to believe in fairy godmothers who made all things right for those who were truly good at heart.

That tender daydream was shattered by the sound of Sarah's wailing. Apparently the lid of her container had worked itself loose and her frog had escaped into the high grass. The distraught child was on her knees hysterically searching the area for any clue of the lucky frog's whereabouts.

"Watch out! Don't step here!" Sarah shrilly commanded to myriad legs passing by.

Hawk's offer to just buy her another one only made her cry more intensely. Shaking her head at his insensitivity, Ella fell to her knees and joined the search. Billy's smug announcement that *his* frog was still safely ensconced in its jar did not help the situation. Though Hawk held out little hope that the critter in question would ever be found, he nonetheless bent down to give the appearance of looking for it.

"You don't understand," Sarah bawled. "I don't want another frog. I want *my* Kermit!"

It was situations just like this that had Hawk tearing out his hair. Clearly the child could no more tell Kermit apart from any other unfortunate amphibian forced to be in this festival. Hawk knew Sarah was only four and a half, but her behavior was so irrational that he didn't know of any other way than bribery to avert a scene that to some outside observer could have all the earmarks of child abuse. He certainly didn't want to end such a lovely day with his daughter tucked beneath his arm screaming her head off as they made their way back to the parking lot, an unfortunate goodly distance away.

"I know you don't want to hear this," he heard Ella tell Sarah in a voice that was both soothing and reasonable. "But maybe it's really for the best. Frogs don't like being cooped up any more than any other wild animal. Maybe it's Kermit's destiny to give some nasty boy warts or to find a princess to kiss him and turn him into a prince or maybe just to find a pretty girl frog and start a great big happy family like yours."

Sarah wiped her eyes with the back of a grimy hand. "You think so?" she asked with a hiccup.

"I do. And I think God would be very happy with you

for letting one of his wild creatures free. I know I'm certainly proud of you.''

''You are?''

Sensing a possible aversion to what only a moment ago seemed certain catastrophe, Hawk chimed in, ''So am I, sweetheart.''

He glanced over his daughter's golden head to give Ella a look of gratitude—and respect. How she managed to avoid disasters with a soft word and a kind tone of voice was a skill he needed to learn. Its advantages over sheer force and/or bribery were obvious not only for the present but also in the future. If he ever hoped to see his children grow into well-mannered, self-reliant young adults, Hawk knew he needed to develop better communication skills himself.

''I don't have to let Rover go, too, do I?'' Billy asked, eyeing both adults nervously.

''Not unless you want to,'' Ella coaxed gently.

''Good!'' he said, sighing in relief and clutching his jar to his chest. Though he wasn't buying the spin Ella put on this predicament, he was nonetheless glad when his little sister stopped crying and his daddy offered to buy them all double-scooped ice cream cones.

''Will you be able to catch a ride home tonight, or do you want to call me to come get you?'' Hawk asked stiffly. As hard as it was to concentrate on anything other than the erotic flick of Ella's tongue as she attacked her ice cream, he hadn't forgotten Buzz's invitation. Not a chance when it had been simmering resentfully on a back burner all day long.

''What are you talking about?'' she asked.

That Ella actually looked perplexed by his question was a bit of balm to his ego. If by some slim chance she had actually forgotten about Buzz's request, Hawk was going to kick himself for reminding her of the party at the lake afterward. Had it not appeared so desperate, he might have actually considered hiring a baby-sitter for the night and accompanying her himself. As a younger man, Hawk had been too busy building his empire to spend much time indulging in keggers and frat parties. From what he heard, he didn't think he'd missed much. Even now the thought of hanging out with a bunch of self-absorbed college kids sounded like as much fun as lancing a boil.

"I'm talking about your friend Buzz's offer to hang out at the lake after the booths shut down."

"Oh, that," Ella replied offhandedly.

"Yes, that."

Hawk thought about expounding. *That disgusting little twerp who implied that he sampled your phenomenal kisses in the past. That infuriating and risky offer to combine drinking and driving with rampant hormones and a decided lack of judgment.*

"I think I'll skip it if you don't mind."

If he didn't mind?

It was all Hawk could do to keep from blowing his suave, aloof cover by breaking out into a toothy grin.

His reaction seemed to prompt an explanation from her. "I've been to my fair share of parties over the years, and to be quite frank, I usually find them a bore."

Indeed the maturity level displayed at such gatherings often left Ella feeling disgusted with many of her peers. The truth was she would much rather spend the remainder of the day falling hopelessly in love with this man.

"Well, if you're sure," Hawk said, interrupting her train of thought. He didn't want to press his luck after all. "I'm ready to go if you are."

No one put up any argument. Hours of sunshine, fattening treats and merriment left them all ready to load up and call it a day. Perhaps it was the thin air, the bright blue sky, or the tops of the mountains glistening in the background that made their time together feel so utterly wonderful. Driving into a deepening sunset that Hawk maintained could not do justice to the color of Ella's hair, they enjoyed breathtaking scenery and the simple pleasure of one another's company on the way home.

Hawk was more relaxed than he had been in a long, long time. He hadn't given thought to business more than once or twice all day. Even the disturbing news that Rover, his son's frog, had staged a daring breakout and was loose somewhere in the car didn't upset him. He simply pulled the vehicle over to the side of the road until the wayward creature was recaptured. Everyone seemed relieved but Sarah. She maintained it was in Rover's best interest to set him free like Kermit, causing her big brother to question whether she had been an accomplice to his escape.

Sideswiped by a sweet wave of sentimentality as she watched Hawk attempt to reason with his children, Ella allowed herself to imagine for a moment what it would be like to be a "real" member of this family. To be a wife. And a mother.

Ella doubted whether Hawk or his children would object to the idea of including her in the family on a purely cerebral level. It was that nagging fear that they were looking for a replacement for the "larger than life" Lauren that sent the butterfly of optimism fluttering out of Ella's grasp. Settling for second best wasn't her style. She might not be as gorgeous, sophisticated or beloved as Hawk's late wife, but that didn't mean Ella didn't see herself as one iota less deserving of happiness.

As the red-eyed sunset surrendered to the purple hues of a perfect summer night, Hawk impetuously reached over and took Ella's hand into his own. The children were too preoccupied in a conversation about providing a safe environment for Rover to pay the act any notice. Given their enthusiastic reaction to the performance their father had given back at the kissing booth, Ella doubted they would have cared. They were happy as long as their father was. And as sad as it was, reality would decree that before long, the children would remember little of their mother but what they heard of her through secondhand sources.

Ella squeezed Hawk's hand back. Their hand holding was in its own way more intimate than all the public or private kisses Hawk had ever bestowed upon her. The simple act of one's fingers entwined with another's conveyed a genuine affection completely separate of sex. Not that Ella had anything against great sex. It was just that intercourse was so often driven purely by physical need that it wasn't something she much trusted. What woman didn't know that promises and sweet words issued in the heat of passion were not always reliable indicators of a man's sincerity?

Holding hands was to Ella's way of thinking incredibly romantic. It made her go tingly all over. And soft inside. And all too vulnerable to the fleeting charm of a moment she intended to press in her memory book like the precious blossoms of some enchanted rose.

Releasing her hand, Hawk proceeded to rub his fingers up and down the length of Ella's arm. She didn't know how something so harmless could be so incredibly sensual. She knew only that, beneath his expert touch, the goose bumps he raised could not have possibly escaped Hawk's notice. Ella was sorry to see the lights of the ranch house glimmer into sight.

Although she remembered leaving the porch light on, she hated to see electricity wasted in other parts of the house. Having lived without public utilities for extended periods of time, such frivolous expense bothered her. She knew Hawk would never broach the subject with the children. He was far more concerned about them growing up without wanting for anything than teaching them the value of thrift. Ella wasn't so sure that wasn't a mistake on his part. Personal experience had taught her that "want" was a great motivator.

By the time they pulled up to the front door, the children had drifted off to sleep in the back seat of the car. Glancing over his shoulder, Hawk cleared his throat in a gesture that Ella was quickly coming to recognize as a nervous harbinger of an uncomfortable subject matter.

"About Buzz," Hawk began, feeling twelve shades an old fool.

"What about him?" Ella asked.

"I know it's none of my business, but…"

That nasty little conjunction sat between them like a piece of stinky cheese.

Valiantly Hawk tried again. "It's just that… I was wondering whether… Listen," he said, plunging his fingers through his hair. "I know there's no place for jealousy in an open relationship such as ours, but something that young man said has been bothering me all day, and I figure it's better to just come out and ask you rather than keep beating around the bush. What exactly did he mean by saying he personally knew the value of your kisses?"

Relieved that it was such a trifling matter, Ella laughed out loud. Hawk could maintain all he wanted that theirs was an open relationship, but the jealousy in his tone made her heart leap within her breast. Never having thought herself the type to inspire possessiveness in anyone, she found herself at a sudden advantage.

"The last time Buzz kissed me," she said in all seriousness, "he knocked me down and literally wrestled it from me."

Hawk's eyes darkened dangerously. His hands clenched the steering wheel in anger. For a delicious moment Ella thought he was going to turn the car around and go after poor Buzz seeking retribution for his crime against womanhood. She hastened to explain.

"We were in first grade as I recall. It was May Day. In case you don't know, the custom around here is that if you receive a May basket from someone of the opposite sex, you are entitled to a kiss in return. In typical tomboy fashion, I resisted tradition and ran away just as fast as I could. It took Buzz the better part of a block to catch me."

"Poor guy," Hawk said, completely without sympathy.

He couldn't resist smiling himself at the thought of Ella only a little older than his own darling Sarah giving all the little boys a run for their money.

"I suppose," he added, "that you kept your father busy at home polishing his shotgun to protect you from such scamps all through school."

"The only thing my father ever polished in regard to me was his exit," Ella assured him.

Hawk was taken aback. He couldn't imagine being estranged from his own children. Ella was so good with them that he had simply assumed she had grown up with the example of two wonderful parents herself.

"You never have told me anything of your background," Hawk prodded gently.

"That's because there's not much to tell," she replied flippantly hoping to let it go at that. Unfortunately the puzzled expression on Hawk's face compelled her to provide him with at least a thumbnail sketch of her pitiful history.

"My biological father ran out on us when Mom told him she was pregnant with me. We didn't have much money, but we had each other and a world full of hopes and dreams. We had several wonderful years together until my mother was diagnosed with cancer. She didn't live much longer. When she died, I was put in an orphanage."

Not a man given to over-sentimentality, Hawk nonetheless felt something hot behind his eyelids. He sucked in his breath and forged bravely onward.

"Surely such a cute little redheaded girl like yourself had no trouble finding a good family to adopt you?" he asked, hoping against hope that he was right.

Ella's bitter laugh assured him that he was not.

"No, but I did pick up some valuable nanny skills from all the foster families in need of free baby-sitting and house cleaning services."

Seeing Hawk's look of horror at the retelling of her life's circumstances, Ella hastened to lighten the mood. She had never intended to tell him this much about herself. The last thing she wanted was for him to start thinking of her as a charity case.

"It turns out it was a good thing. Those skills certainly have come in handy lately."

Unable to respond to such cheerfulness in light of the dismal facts revealed, Hawk took one hand off the steering wheel and reached over to squeeze Ella's hand reassuringly. His heart contracted in pain to think of her orphaned so young. Assuredly that was why she was so compassionate and insightful in dealing with two motherless children desperate for a woman's touch in their lives.

Aware that Ella was deliberately downplaying the more painful elements of her past, he didn't press her further.

He knew only too well that a person had to deal with grief in his or her own way.

Hawk gently awakened the children, then came around the car to open the door for Ella. The simple gesture made her feel like a princess alighting from a golden carriage. It didn't matter that Ella knew just how dangerous such fanciful thinking could be. It was beyond her power to keep hope from resting on her shoulders.

It wasn't completely out of the question to think life might actually write her a fairy-tale ending, was it?

Those beautiful sand castles she had been building in her mind came crashing down about her the minute they opened the front door and discovered exactly why all the lights were burning at home.

Nine

"**A**unt Frannie!" cried the children, shaking off the remnants of sleep and blasting past Ella in a blur.

Lounging upon the living room couch was the most beautiful woman she had ever seen. When Sarah had mentioned her Aunt Frannie before, Ella had pictured a more matronly personage. This femme fatale reminded her of a blond Cleopatra holding court. Wearing a silk chemise and matching robe of an exquisite design, she set her wineglass down to throw her arms open wide. The welcome the children gave their aunt spoke of their genuine affection for her.

Hawk also greeted his sister-in-law with a big smile and a warm hug that lasted far too long to suit Ella. Clearly this relative's favored standing in the family hadn't been diminished any by Lauren's death. A petite five-foot-three-inches on tiptoes, his ex-sister-in-law barely reached Hawk's shoulders. Perhaps that was why she didn't see Ella standing in the shadows awaiting a formal introduction.

Digging her bloodred nails into Hawk's back, she exclaimed in a breathless, feminine way, "Don't squeeze me too hard! You big men sometimes forget your strength."

Even though Ella didn't actually know the woman herself, she wanted to squeeze her, too—around the neck.

"What are you doing here?" the children demanded, jumping up and down in their excitement. "How long can you stay?"

Her smile was beatific as she answered their questions with a distinctly theatrical flair. "Your Aunt Frannie is here to be your nanny for as long as you need me!"

Ella felt the bottom drop out of her stomach. To be replaced by this ravishing creature was too cruel. Why couldn't Aunt Frannie weigh closer to two hundred pounds and have a nasal quality to her voice instead of such an intriguing lilt? Why didn't Aunt Frannie stay where she belonged like New York or Paris or wherever it was that she bought those dazzling clothes?

Why did life always pull the rug out from under Ella whenever she got her hopes up?

Frannie's announcement seemed to have been met with stunned disbelief. Having expected a more enthusiastic response to her offer, her voice took on an injured quality. "Have I said something wrong?" she asked.

"Not at all," Hawk hastened to assure her. "We're just surprised to see you. After all, the outback of Wyoming isn't exactly your typical getaway destination."

Frannie's response was a throaty laugh. "Indeed not, but when you called and said your nanny ran off, leaving you single-handedly responsible for my nephew and niece as well as your demanding business, I dropped everything, abandoned civilization and rushed right out to help.''

"That's very kind of you, Frannie," Hawk began, "but—"

Billy cut him off. "But we already have a nanny. Ella!" he said pointing to the shadows of the foyer.

Running to the door, he dragged her into the circle of soft light illuminating the room. Self-consciously Ella wiped her hands on the seat of her ragged cutoffs. If ever there was a question about who was the real princess among them, Frannie answered it with a royal sweep of her pale blue eyes.

"Where did you ever find such a charming creature?" she asked.

At the moment Ella felt about as charming as a snake publicly shedding its skin. Nonetheless, she extended her hand politely and received, in return, a tepid, limp fish handshake. For all the sweetness Aunt Frannie was exuding for her relations, Ella sensed an undercurrent of hostility.

"This is Ella McBride, the young woman I hired to watch over the children," Hawk said. "I thought I e-mailed you about her."

Ella cringed at the indifferent description. Not that she expected him to announce that they were lovers or anything. Still, she found herself wishing that he would simply come and stand beside her.

Frannie waved a jeweled hand at Hawk. "I'm afraid I'm just as bad not keeping up with my e-mail as I ever was with snail mail."

He smiled indulgently as one would at a forgetful but adorable child. "Ella, this is Lauren's sister, Frannie. She has been a godsend to us all. I doubt if I could have made it through Lauren's death without her help."

The look of gratitude he wore was so real that it left no doubt whatsoever of his sincerity. "If I haven't told you enough, Fran, I can never repay you for all you've done for us. The fact that you would put your own life on hold to volunteer your time to take care of Billy, Sarah and me means more than you'll ever know."

"Oh, stop!" she told him.

The flush lingering upon those high patrician cheekbones was telling. Clearly the woman wanted more from Hawk than gratitude alone. Ella wondered if he was aware of the sexual tension crackling in the room like static electricity. The striking resemblance between Frannie and the pictures Ella had seen of Lauren was unnerving. She wondered what memories his ex-sister-in-law's presence brought back for Hawk. What mixed feelings it evoked?

Gratefulness? Guilt? Grief?

Ella spied all of them in Hawk's eyes as he continued gazing at Frannie.

"Just 'cuz Ella's taking care of us, doesn't mean you can't stay," Sarah said, tugging at her aunt's silken sleeve.

"I don't know, honey," Frannie said, bending down to look the child in the eye. "I'm not so sure I wouldn't be in the way."

Everyone but Ella looked offended at the thought. "You know you're always welcome here. Just because we're not in the market for a servant doesn't mean we're not delighted to see you," Hawk reassured her.

"Then you really don't mind my dropping by uninvited?" Her voice was a cultivated, sultry breeze.

"Of course not. We have plenty of room and would love for you to stay as long as you'd like. Really."

A perfect smile replaced the worry lines furrowing her delicate brow. "In that case, I'd be thrilled to spend some time getting reacquainted with my favorite niece and nephew.''

The children squealed happily. They looked as delighted with their aunt's pronouncement as she looked relieved to hear her duties would be limited to being a ''good time'' auntie. Ella didn't think those manicured nails would fare well under soapy dishwater, modeling clay or finger paints.

''Would you be a dear and put my things in the bedroom next to Hawk's?'' she asked turning to Ella. Though her smile failed to crinkle her eyes, it did remain in place for a painful twenty seconds.

Indignation burned beneath the surface of Ella's fair skin. Having just been bluntly reminded that she was merely a *servant*, she assumed a proper servile attitude and reached for the top bag on a mountain of luggage.

''Wouldn't you rather I put you in the guest room down the hall?'' she asked pleasantly. ''It's got a wonderful view of both the creek and the aspen grove.''

The suggestion warranted a condescending look from Frannie and an emphatic shake of her blond curls. Clearly Hawk's ex-sister-in-law was more concerned with a view of his backside rather than the countryside.

''Let me help you with those bags,'' he told Ella, grabbing a couple by the handles. The muscles of his arms bunched appealingly beneath the load.

''Don't do me any favors,'' Ella hissed under her breath.

Hawk looked surprised by her sudden animosity. He seemed as clueless about hurting her feelings as he appeared oblivious to the fact that Frannie was surreptitiously ogling him. Ella felt a twinge of guilt. Never in her life had she acted ungraciously toward a fellow wayfarer. She often noted that the smaller the house, the greater the hospitality. Indeed, in her own tiny cabin, many was the time she had played hostess to a stranded traveler, a friend down on her luck, or an acquaintance who simply needed time away from the pressure of a hectic lifestyle and strained relationships. Over the years her humble home had been a haven for anyone who happened to stumble upon it—a magical cottage according to Billy and Sarah. Thus, it came as a surprise to Ella herself to realize that she wanted to pitch Aunt Frannie and her expensive hand-tooled Italian luggage out the front door.

Unexpected tears pooled in her eyes. Tears she was determined to hide from her employer as she dumped her first load of baggage in the bedroom next to his.

"What is the matter?" he asked as she jostled past him on her way back to pick up her second load.

"Nothing," she said in a tone that indicated otherwise.

Hawk grabbed her by the arm. "Like hell!" he countered.

Ella drew herself to her full height, put her hands on her hips, and assumed a fighting stance. "Maybe you'd rather I put her Highness's things in your room and spare you the trouble of ten extra steps!"

Had she not been a woman, Ella suspected Hawk would have flattened her on the spot.

"Such a vile remark is unlike you," he said.

His voice was cold and his eyes hard. Clearly Hawk was hurt and as perplexed by her outburst as Ella was about Frannie's intrusion. She thought even his words had taken on an unpleasant high-brow quality since he'd discovered Frannie under his roof.

"I'll have you know," he continued, "that woman's been here for this family. Fran stayed by her sister's bedside the entire time she was hospitalized. Day and night she remained by Lauren's side, giving comfort and support to all of us, arranging for Billy's and Sarah's well-being and helping them cope with the most tragic loss in any child's life.''

That remark got to Ella like none other could. Remembering how desperately she could have used a friend or relative when her own mother passed away, she fought back the surge of regret for making such an uncharitable remark. Unlike Billy and Sarah, she'd had no one at all to stand by her or offer to help rebuild her life.

Hawk ignored the pained expression on her face. ''Not only is your comment unbecoming of a lady, it is also totally unfounded. For God's sake, what must you think of me to imply I'd carry on with my dead wife's sister?''

Ella took a step back. It was the maddest she had ever seen Hawk, and though he had never given her any cause to fear him, she had been around men who lashed out at far less. Guilt loosened the gnarled hand of jealousy twisting her guts into a knot. That she owed Hawk an apology only made it that much more difficult to admit she might be wrong.

Why couldn't he understand how it hurt her to be shoved aside like a day-old newspaper now that the latest, glossy edition had arrived on his doorstep? The scene smacked of all the old painful memories of being passed over again and again for adoption. It seemed fate was determined to keep throwing those beautiful blue eyed blondes in her face throughout her lifetime. If a prospective parent couldn't see past her freckles and gawkiness, how could she possibly expect a man like William Fawson Hawk III to consider her for his wife?

Ella tried swallowing past the huge lump lodged in her throat.

''Your *servant* has been duly reprimanded for her unseemly demeanor,'' she told him with a pert salute before straining toward sincerity. "I certainly didn't mean to slight the memory of your wife or imply that you have something going on with your sister-in-law. I'm sure she is a lovely person."

Despite her words, Ella had taken an automatic dislike to the woman. As far as she was concerned, her speech was overblown, her manners condescending, and, despite everything Hawk said to the contrary, her attitude blatantly self-centered. She could see that Hawk was genuinely perplexed by her mood swing. She wished she could explain that this was an altogether hideous ending to what had otherwise been the most perfect day of her life. The last thing she needed was Saint Frannie to remind her that she had no business giving even a second's worth of credibility to the fantasy she'd been building in her mind— the one in which the devilishly handsome, wealthy man falls in love with the lowly minion of the castle.

As opposed to simply bedding her at his convenience and moving on.

It had been stupid on her part to hope for anything more. The rich married the rich, and the poor, if they were lucky, were allowed to serve the cake at their weddings. Although Hawk was adamant about having no desire to hook up romantically with his ex-sister-in-law, Ella had seen the glint in Frannie's eyes and knew the predatory blonde was not at all opposed to the idea herself.

"This might be a good time to review my job description," she said stiffly, doing her best to keep her tears at bay. For a woman who never had much all her life, Ella's pride was always in reserve. "Am I to be Aunt Frannie's personal handmaid as well as your children's nanny?"

Hawk looked startled. All of a sudden his eyes lost the look of flint her earlier remark had put there. A smile flitted across his features as he tipped her face up by the stubborn set of her chin.

"Is that what this is all about?" he asked, looking relieved that he had stumbled upon the answer. "You are nobody's servant, Ella. I thought you knew that you are a part of this family."

Her stupid tears refused to do as they were told. As they welled over and spilled down her cheeks, Ella cursed Hawk's kind words.

"And as such," he told her, kissing away those runaway tears, "I expect you to treat Fran like you would one of your own relations. I know she can be a little demanding at times, but she really is good at heart."

"How can I treat her like one of my own when I don't have any relatives?" she asked petulantly.

"None?" he asked, wincing at the thought of her having faced the world all alone for so very long.

"Nary an aunt, uncle, or cousin twice removed. You know, I've always dreamed of being part of a real family, not just a castaway floating from foster home to foster home." Ella gave him a weak smile then brightened suddenly. "Maybe if I try thinking of her nibs as an eccentric relative, one suffering under delusions of grandeur, we could learn to tolerate one another. That is, as long as you promise to explain to her that I wasn't put on earth to wait on her hand and foot."

Hawk smiled and took her into his arms. "Done!" he pronounced, holding her against the beating of his heart.

He felt a sudden fierce desire to protect this blithe spirit against a world too cruel. When he squeezed her reassuringly, she clung to him, wrapping her arms around the strong column of his neck and pressing her curves against him. Hawk reacted in a purely masculine, involuntary way that caused both hope and desire to rise in Ella's breast.

"You smell like summer," he remarked, breathing in the essence of her hair.

The fragrance of ambergris that she had dotted along her pulse lines earlier in the day did indeed evoke thoughts of the seashore at summer. As did those foam-green eyes of hers glistening as he lowered his head to hers. Sighing, Ella opened her lips in expectation of a kiss that would make everything all better.

"What *is* keeping you, Hawk?" a mellifluous voice called from the other room.

Ella's eyes flew open as she felt Hawk stiffen. Frannie couldn't have ruined the moment more effectively had she thrown a bucket of icy water upon them.

"I'll be right there," Hawk called. Glad to have reestablished peace in his own home, he placed a chaste kiss upon Ella's forehead as he stepped out of her embrace. "Don't worry. I promise to have a little talk with Frannie before I turn in tonight."

Ella was tempted to rub off the spot of warmth lingering upon her skin. How could she ever hope to maintain any emotional distance when such a restrained peck had the power to brand her as his forever?

"I'll tuck the children in and give you two time to catch up," she told him, swallowing her pride and pasting on a cheery smile.

"Do we *have* to go to bed already?" the children asked a few minutes later when the edict came down. The inflection in their voices verged on whining.

Ella settled the matter by issuing what she considered a reasonable compromise. "Yes, you *have* to go to bed, but you're welcome to wake your auntie up first thing in the morning after you've all had a good night's sleep."

She hoped Her Highness was used to rising shortly after the sun did. Satisfied, the children allowed her to read them a nighttime story, listen to their prayers, and turn on their night-lights. She listened patiently while tucking them into bed as they chattered excitedly about their visitor. By the time Ella slipped exhausted into her own bed, Hawk and Frannie were deep into conversation and an aged bottle of wine their guest had provided.

The "little talk" Hawk had promised lasted hours. It was agony for Ella to lay between the sheets and listen to the sound of their voices, which were alternately sprinkled with loud bursts of laughter that made her want to bury her head beneath her pillow. She found their hushed tones even more disturbing. That she was overtired didn't help her find sleep any more quickly.

Home had been an elusive concept in her life since the death of her mother. That Ella had come to feel at home under Hawk's protective roof was a big step for her emotionally. Tonight, however, those feelings of belonging evaporated as she felt herself transported back to a time when she was bounced from one foster home to another like a human Superball. Most of the bedrooms where she had spent her youth were small, dingy rooms jammed full of bunk beds and other foster care children intended to generate income for the host family. Ella remembered one room in particular. It smelled of wet carpet that never completely dried out from periodic sewage leaks. It was a basement room with no windows and only a bare bulb to illuminate her homework. Her host parents were absent much of the time and expected her to look after their own children who had lovely rooms upstairs. After weeks of crying herself to sleep, Ella finally summoned the courage to complain to her social worker about her living conditions. He said to be grateful and keep her mouth shut.

The exact opposite of that spiteful room had been one decorated in yellow floral wallpaper. The window above her canopy bed had matching white eyelet curtains that shifted in the breeze. Every night Ella got down on her knees beside that bed and begged God to make this home permanent. The kind couple who had taken her in were considering formally adopting her. However, when the wife became pregnant after years of infertility, Ella found herself helping the woman transform her lovely bedroom into a nursery for the baby.

Having learned the hard way that blood is thicker than water, Ella berated herself for forgetting it. As wonderful as it was, this home was not hers and never would be. The two people conversing in the other room were connected by history and a bloodline and a social structure that someone like Ella could never hope to penetrate. Outcasts such as herself would do well to remember not to get too attached to romantic fantasies or flesh-and-blood children who would likely forget her just as soon as their daddy remarried someone of their class.

"Too late," trilled the meadowlark outside her window. *"Too late, you silly little fool...."*

Ten

Maneuvering around Mount Saint Frannie seemed as easy to Ella as dusting the Statue of Liberty had it been located in one's living room. Having lived at Red Feather Ranch for nearly a month, Ella had come to think of it as her second home. Their new houseguest seemed intent on remedying Ella's false sense of security. Putting the nanny in her place was uppermost in their houseguest's mind whether by testing every cranny for dust, asking for special dietary consideration, or questioning Ella's methodology with the children. Under her breath, Ella referred to Frannie as high-maintenance company.

"Would you be a dear and make me a sunrise latte with a spot of hazelnut cream? Decaffeinated, of course, with just a smidgen of whipped cream on top," Frannie demanded upon tumbling out of bed.

As promised, the children had awakened their aunt at the crack of dawn. Ella suspected Frannie wasn't accus-

tomed to seeing daylight before brunch was typically
growing cold, but she wasn't harsh in the least with the
children for disturbing her beauty rest. In fact, when she
emerged from her bedroom an hour or so later, she looked
like she had just stepped off the society page.

Frannie's blond hair was fine and spilled around her
shoulders like sunshine. Ella wondered if she had it light-
ened professionally or if it was naturally beautiful. She
pushed a heavy strand of her own thick hair out of her
eyes. It was, she knew from school-day taunts, the color
of carrots.

"I'll be glad to get you a cup of coffee left over from
breakfast," Ella told her, putting down the book she was
in the midst of reading to the children to do Frannie's
bidding.

She disappeared into the kitchen, returning a moment
later with the coffee, a carton of cream and a Danish
heated in the microwave. Frannie sniffed at the offering
like Hissy Face showing her disgust.

"Thank you, dear," she purred, her voice a study in
upper class tonation. She nibbled delicately on the edge
of the Danish and merely wrinkled her nose at the coffee.

"You're welcome."

Thinking of this woman as a long-lost relative did little
to quash Ella's desire to throttle her. She had changed out
of her Paris peignoir into what Ella assumed could only
be categorized as "lounging around with nothing better
to do wear." The woman clearly had a penchant for silk.
The soft yellow material reminded Ella of butterfly wings.
She longed to reach out and touch it herself, but worried
her rough fingers would snag the fine cloth. Her own
wardrobe was shameful in comparison. In addition to the
shorts, T-shirts and sweats she had worn every day in
place of the white maid's uniform their houseguest

seemed to expect, Ella owned only two dresses for social occasions. Her pajamas consisted of an oversize T-shirt, and in the winter, she staved off the cold with a pair of long johns.

Frannie abandoned her breakfast and picked up the book Ella had set down. "If you wouldn't mind hanging up my things, I'll just take up reading where you left off," she told her with a dismissive wave of her jeweled hand.

Ella did mind. Very much, in fact, but she said nothing that would indicate how much it hurt her to see the children clamber into their aunt's silken lap. Having never had the benefit of close relatives, she understood the sanctity of maintaining that special bond. Whatever else one could say about Frannie, it was clear that the affection she felt for her nephew and niece was real. Ella could not begrudge them that.

It took over an hour to hang up and fold all the lovely clothes that Frannie had packed. Wherever she thought she was going to wear a silver-sequined evening gown in Backwater, Wyoming, was beyond Ella, but she indulged some of her own fantasies by holding the shimmering masterpiece up to herself in the mirror. Certain that such a gown looked better on Frannie's more angular, model-like figure than her own, she relegated it to a hanger with a sigh. The price tag indicated not only that it had yet to be worn but also that the cost was more than Ella could even imagine spending on an entire wardrobe, let alone one unpractical dress, no matter who designed it.

Later in the day she packed the children their usual picnic lunch in hopes of leaving their aunt behind with something more palatable than bologna sandwiches. Looking forward to some time away from their house-guest's demands, Ella was dismayed when Frannie volunteered to "give her some time alone" thereby neatly

substituting herself in Ella's place. Apparently serious
about getting down and dirty with the children, she had
changed out of her silken concoction into a pair of twill
pants and a matching angora sweater that Ella knew cost
more than a month of waitressing wages could buy. Hawk
joined them at the creek as Ella took her own sandwich
to her room where she proceeded to add a wicked queen
to a painting she was working on. That she was blonde
with a figure like a cigarette was no coincidence.

Dinner proved to be a strained affair. Frannie insisted
that Ella set the big dining table rather than eating at the
kitchen table as was their custom. She also firmly requested the use of the good china, which had grown
"shamefully" dusty in the antique buffet cabinet.

"What's the use of saving it for a rainy day?" she
asked, waving her arms about as if she were throwing
confetti. Clearly every day was a party day wherever
Frannie went. "Where we come from, presentation is just
as important as the preparation of the food itself," she
told Ella.

"Umm," Ella responded, assuming by the plural "we"
that Frannie meant Hawk and herself. She didn't much
appreciate feeling like she was being tutored in Snobbery
101. "Where I come from, it's just about having enough
to eat period."

Frannie looked startled by the very idea. Throughout
dinner she had Ella jumping up every other mouthful to
retrieve something or another from the kitchen. Every
time Ella tried to sit down, it seemed Frannie would remember something else vital to the presentation of the
meal.

"You know, darling," she said to Hawk over the clink
of her cut glass wine goblet. "If you're not careful Billy

and Sarah will turn into barbarians out here in the wilds of Wyoming.''

That well placed *darling* cut sharper than the knife with which Hawk used to carve the roast Ella had cooked. Never before had she felt the desire to plunge an eating utensil into another woman's heart. She had originally planned on fixing a casserole for dinner, but Frannie had looked so truly aghast at the thought of actually being asked to consume such peasant food that Ella gave in to her request for a more suitable cuisine. She had never known anyone to turn up his nose at homemade roast, potatoes, carrots and fresh peach cobbler, but then she'd never been around anyone like Aunt Frannie before. As usual their houseguest's compliments were saccharine, but her body language indicated that she may as well have been asked to sit down to dinner in the company of lumberjacks hunkered down around a stump with nary a napkin between them.

''Mind you,'' she began, ''it's not that I find it boring out here. Your home is utterly charming, Hawk, really it is. Now that I've seen it for myself, I can honestly see why you would choose to uproot your family and move them to such an idyllic setting. I just worry that the children are going to become so isolated here that they might lose those crucial social skills Lauren worked so hard to instill in them.''

Ella gritted her teeth. It wasn't up to her to point out that in a short while they would be enrolled in school and would have many opportunities to mix with other children of all social spheres. She was grateful when Hawk made the same observation.

''Public school?'' Frannie gasped, almost spilling her wine upon the recently starched tablecloth. ''You can't possibly be serious.''

Hawk arched an eyebrow at his sister-in-law. "Does it help to know that I'm the product of a public school education?" he asked.

In light of the delicate cough that was her only response, he did his best to allay her fears. "Will it make you feel better if I promise to look into private schooling?" Hawk asked her.

Ella had a feeling the only thing that would suffice for Frannie was some exclusive boarding school far, far away. One with a pretentious curriculum and administrators forced to cater to parents who had a problem saying no to their children. She beat back the sense of outrage that thought evoked by reminding herself that she was only planning on staying long enough to pay her way through college. Certainly no one had ever implied this was going to be a permanent gig. If the thought of Billy and Sarah being shipped away to some snooty boarding school left a gaping hole in her heart, she would do well to remember that as an outsider she had no say in their upbringing.

"Need I remind you, Hawk, that you could very well sell your company, enjoy the fruits of your labor and live very comfortably without the headaches of running a company from the boonies?" Frannie asked.

As Hawk started to shake his head, she held up her hands to stop him from offering his standard explanation. "I know, I know," she said, nonplused at his insistence that work gave life purpose. "If you're bound and determined to make a go of it here, I've got a suggestion. I really would like to make myself useful around here and earn my keep in some small way or another."

Ella held her breath. It was hard enough trying to work around this woman when she was reveling in the role of pampered houseguest. She could only imagine what it would be like to assist her in some outside project. Exhausted from a long day of cooking and cleaning and waiting on Frannie, not to mention taking care of the children in her spare time, Ella wanted nothing more than to clear the dishes and fall into bed.

"I'd like to throw you all a housewarming party. From what Billy and Sarah tell me, they are virtual strangers with their neighbors—their young nanny being the one notable exception."

She turned to Ella with what appeared to be genuine interest. "The children tell me your home is charming. You'll have to give me a tour some day."

Ella doubted Frannie would allow her registered pets to board in such a humble abode. The thought of actually entertaining her there was enough to conjure up images of the Mad Hatter's tea party. She tried to suppress a laugh at the thought.

"In any case, as I said, if you insist in living in such a remote place, Hawk, I think it would behoove you to meet some of the more influential people in the area. I'm sure there have to be some prominent ranchers and businessmen around who have children of their own with whom Billy and Sarah can associate. Surely you're not the only eccentric millionaire running his company out here via modern technology. I understand the tax structure in this state is most advantageous. Perhaps we could even find a potential client or two hidden in the woodwork. Maybe I can honestly contribute something while I'm here."

Hawk looked bored with her suggestion that he mingle more. He had never struck Ella as a social climber, but then again she was sure he hadn't achieved such incredible success by being shy and introverted either.

"Maybe I could rustle you up a rodeo star or two," Ella offered dryly.

"Could you, dear?" Frannie gushed, completely unaware that the offer had been tongue in cheek. "That would be certain to provide some fascinating conversation. And maybe you could ask a couple of your more well-known artist friends to join us."

"This isn't exactly Greenwich Village," Ella told her without malice, "but I can always find a handful of starving artists who would love a free meal." Phoebe immediately came to mind. Not only was she dying to meet the mysterious man for whom Ella was working, she was also sure to prove the life of the party. Not that the hostess was likely to surrender that title easily herself.

"This really is not necessary, Fran," Hawk interrupted, noting the look of horror on her face at Ella's suggestion that she include a ragamuffin group of hippies on her guest list. "As much as I appreciate your intentions, I don't think that—"

He didn't finish his thought. The disappointment shimmering in his sister-in-law's blue eyes was enough to make him reconsider. "I don't think that you're going to find too many takers. This country is notoriously short on pretentiousness and long on independent thinkers."

"Just the kind of men I prefer," Frannie cooed. "Quite frankly, I've grown bored with the boy toys in our set back home."

Hawk gave her an inquisitive look. "Are you actually thinking of settling down then?"

Frannie snapped her manicured fingers in front of his face. "In a heartbeat—if I were to find the right man."

Ella thought she might heave what little of her dinner she had eaten. One would have to be completely thick-skulled to miss Frannie's meaning. Clearly she wanted nothing more than to slip into her departed sister's bed slippers. The only one present unaware of her not so subtle meaning was Hawk himself.

"In that case, I'd be more than happy to have you plan as elaborate a party as you want. I bet Ella wouldn't mind helping you either." He smiled as benevolently as a king granting the court permission to plan a ball.

I'll bet you're wrong, she longed to say. Of course, this was neither the time nor the place to act as the fly in the proverbial ointment which was likely why Frannie had made the suggestion at the dinner table with everyone present. Ella determined to make her feelings known to Hawk in a more private setting. Still, if there was any possibility that this shindig would hasten Frannie's departure or preoccupy her time so that she had little inclination to continue pestering Ella, she was all for it.

After doing a mountain of dishes, Ella announced that she was going to turn in early. No one tried to stop her. Frannie looked positively delighted by the prospect of tucking in her nephew and niece herself not to mention spending the remainder of the evening with Hawk. Ella was sorely disappointed that he didn't bother stopping in to kiss her good-night, leaving her to wonder whether she had only imagined what they had shared just a few days ago.

Had she been able to keep her eyelids open, she would have discovered him standing in her doorway observing her sleeping form with a look of undisguised tenderness on his face. Frannie caught it quite by accident herself.

It had taken all her womanly wiles to entertain Hawk throughout the evening and stop him from assisting the hired help. Part of the reason she was so drawn to the man was the unmanicured edges that remained from his middle class roots. Unable to recognize a diamond in the rough, Lauren had struggled to make Hawk into something he wasn't—a social dandy. If given half a chance, Frannie vowed not to make the same mistake. Her sister had been a fool running around on her husband with simpering Romeos who couldn't compare to a real man like Hawk. After all, self-made millionaires with bodies to die for didn't come along every day. That Hawk was more concerned about providing for his family and maintaining living wages for everyone on his staff meant far more to her than which fork he used at dinner.

And so it was when she rounded the corner on some trumped up excuse to run into Hawk wearing her most elegant lingerie and saw him standing in Ella's doorway like some moonstruck adolescent, Frannie knew she had to act fast. She'd be damned if she was going to be bested by an ill-educated servant with the social connections of a gnat. Once upon a time in his life, Hawk married her beautiful but shallow older sister not only because he loved her but also in hopes of advancing himself socially. Having accomplished all that he had with a woman who hadn't believed in him, Frannie couldn't imagine what he could do with a supportive, well-connected wife at his side. But she had every intention of finding out.

Eleven

From the cold reception Ella received from Frannie the following day, she could only assume that Hawk had spoken to her about laying off the orders. She could only assume because Frannie seemed even more intent than before to keep Hawk to herself. Ella considered it a mixed blessing. Their houseguest was so into planning her gala that she left Ella and the children alone for great blocks of time. On the down side, she was glued to Hawk's side needing his constant attention. Ella couldn't remember the last time they had been able to steal a moment alone.

She caught sight of him on her way out the door after breakfast dishes were cleared and put away. He shot her a look of dismay over his morning paper as if to say "Don't leave me!" as Frannie shoved a sheaf of ideas at him. Ella suppressed a giggle. Apparently she wasn't alone in not understanding the importance of presentation regarding the food, theme and invitations of a party.

"I'm taking the kids down to the creek to fish," she told Hawk, hoping to make a fleet-footed exit before Frannie had a chance to detain her with a long list of chores. "Would either of you like to come along?"

Frannie shuddered.

"I'd love to," Hawk rejoined.

His eyes held her gaze across the space of the room. Without another word exchanged, he conveyed a sense of longing that left Ella breathless. *I miss you!* echoed in the clash of their eyes. Ella felt her heart trip over her silent tongue. How she longed to tempt him with a blanket spread out beneath the branches of a cottonwood and a sky as blue as cornflowers.

Frannie intercepted the look which passed between them with one that narrowed her own eyes.

"He can't possibly," she told Ella, sounding rather like his mother. "Not with everything we have to plan, but you go on and run along. I'm sure you and the children will all have a great time."

There was no mistaking the way in which she deliberately chose to lump Ella into the same category of a teenage baby-sitter just a few years older than her charges. Ella resisted the urge to stick her thumb in her mouth and play the farcical comment to the hilt. Perhaps it would be more fitting if she merely stuck her tongue out in a fitting juvenile protest. Instead she chose to punish her acerbic guest with a smile and a promise.

"Hopefully we'll catch enough to make a nice mess for dinner."

Hawk laughed at the horrified expression on Frannie's face and explained that the term mess was a colloquialism that had nothing to do with dirty messes whatsoever.

Ella caught a final snatch of their conversation as she headed outside to where Billy was struggling with a shovel to unearth enough worms to keep the fish jumping for hours.

"And don't you forget gold diggers come in all ages and shapes," Frannie said a little too loudly.

Ella was tempted to point out that most gold diggers didn't use actual shovels to dig up night crawlers but decided it wasn't worth her energy. If Hawk didn't know her any better than that, chances were he never would. Instead she decided to focus her attention on the excited faces of the two children she had promised to take fishing. Tucking her sketch pad under her arm, she led them across the meadow to a beaver pond that looked promising.

A cover of clouds and a gentle breeze kept the day from being too hot. Having caught many a meal this way herself, Ella was not in the least squeamish about baiting a hook. She positioned the children on either side of her. They enjoyed each other's company in the shade of a rocky inlet. Ella opened her sketchbook and immersed herself in drawing a bottle-blue dragonfly competing with a pair of butterflies for a branch of honeysuckle.

The sight of a beautiful young woman helping his children catch their first fish caused Hawk's eyes to cloud up. He thought about offering to let them use his heart as bait since Ella had single-handedly reeled that fighter in herself. She was presently engaged in shinnying up an ill-fated elm to release Sarah's hook from an overhanging limb. With the sunlight spilling around her shoulders turning her hair the color of burnished copper, she seemed to him an angel. Why God would send a man as world-weary as Hawk a divine intercessor he'd never know. Right now it was enough to simply appreciate heaven-sent gifts.

"I caught one! I caught one!" cried Billy, reeling for all he was worth.

A minute later he was holding up an eight-inch brook trout that most grown anglers would have tossed back. Hawk suspected, however, that it would take a brave man indeed to wrestle that trophy from his son's little hands.

"Nice job, son," he called from behind them, startling Ella so that she almost fell out of her tree.

She clambered down from her precarious perch. "Glad you could make it after all," she hollered out, watching him lumber down the hill in a red T-shirt and a pair of jeans that made him seem a native born and bred. It seemed impossible that Hawk was as comfortable in a boardroom as he was in this mountain setting. Overhead his namesake flew in a wide circle with his mate surveying all that was his.

"I wouldn't have missed it for the world," he said. "Moments like these are exactly why I left Chicago in the first place."

His gaze was warm upon her as she swung from a low branch and landed on the ground in front of him. Rather like a ripe peach, he thought, surveying a worn pair of shorts that did wonders for her delightfully rounded figure. Hawk felt a twinge of guilt that he'd never paid her limited and, as Frannie put it, "deplorable" wardrobe much attention. He recalled her pointed remarks. *It simply won't do to have your hired help running around looking like Daisy Mae. What will people think?*

Probably that he was a cheap son of a gun who didn't pay well. He promised to remedy the situation immediately.

"Oooh, oooh!" cried Sarah who had just realized the worm she had retrieved from the bait can was cold and wiggly.

Hawk and Ella shared a laugh at her expense. Her feminine pout would have done her Aunt Frannie proud.

"Can you stay a while?" Ella asked over the hammering of her heart. This was the first opportunity the two of them had had to be together without Frannie's surveillance since their guest had appeared on the scene, and Ella's body was reacting as if they were completely alone and naked. Despite the inappropriateness of her thoughts, she couldn't help but let her gaze drift to the blanket she had spread on the ground earlier for the picnic to come. She suddenly had a better idea how to implement that comfy old quilt.

"You have no idea just how much I'd like that," Hawk told her with a rueful shake of his head. "But the truth of the matter is Frannie sent me here on a mission. It's not exactly a position I relish either."

Ella crooked a wicked eyebrow at him. "Did I just hear you say something about a missionary position?"

Realizing that she had actually blurted out the bawdy remark, she blushed. The sound of Hawk's laughter echoed off the mountain walls and resonated in the chambers of an ever-expanding heart.

"Now there's a proposition intended to knock a man's socks off," he said. "I have to admit I'm never surprised by what comes out of those adorable Kewpie doll lips. If I don't get to finger paint with you again soon, I think I'll explode."

Ella pursed those aforementioned lips at him and blew him a kiss. Even though her heart was reacting like someone had just shot her full of adrenaline, she assumed he was only toying with her. If anything, her lips, like her figure, were a little too full to be fashionable. Once, a woman she didn't even know asked her if she availed herself of collagen injections. The only other notable re-

mark anyone ever made about her lips was that they sometimes moved too much. Years of being "shushed" by
child service organizations and adults in charge had taught
her to be less boisterous. Considering the fact that no one
seemed willing to listen to her anyway, Ella had thought
it a valuable lesson. It was just too bad that it was one
she couldn't master.

At the moment she was just happy to be flirting with
Hawk. Since Frannie's entry into their lives, Ella had begun to wonder if he even remembered she was alive. Unfortunately, their present circumstances were hardly suited
to the kind of romantic flings idealized in the media.
Aside from being pestered by horseflies the size of a
thumb, the children needed constant attention. Between
rebaiting hooks, untangling line and unhooking snags
there wasn't enough time to sneak in a kiss let alone
something more decadent upon the quilt spread on the
ground.

"Frannie wants to take the children to town to find
them some clothes for the party. Since it's Wednesday
and your art class day, I thought you might want to take
the afternoon off and do some shopping yourself. I want
you to buy yourself some nice clothes—on me," he hastened to add. Hawk wasn't sure why he expected Ella to
protest, but he had noticed she spent very little of her
paycheck on herself. Was she saving up for something
special? Surely she couldn't have too many bills accu-
mulated of her own.

"Pick up some suitable clothes for everyday interactions with the children and find yourself something special
for the party. I want you to feel comfortable."

When he pulled his credit card from his wallet, Ella felt
conflicted. She was thrilled to actually be invited to the
ball rather than being relegated to baby-sitting in the base-

ment. Ella suspected that if Frannie had her way, she would be assigned to sit at the children's table in the kitchen for the duration of the party. However, the use of the word "suitable" implied that he was displeased with her shoddy wardrobe. Ashamed at the thought that he might be embarrassed to be seen with her in public, Ella tilted her chin proudly in the air and considered refusing his offer outright. Didn't he know that she was more than the clothes she wore? Still, she really didn't want to throw his generosity back in his face. When the universe opened up its arms and offered her a gift, she had learned to accept it graciously. The thought of actually shopping for herself without worrying about the cost was something out of a childhood fantasy. She squinted at Hawk.

"You look more like a hairy godmother than a fairy one," she remarked.

When Hawk smiled, the warmth of it soaked into her very bones. To be thus pampered was such a foreign concept to her that she couldn't help but be the teeniest bit skeptical about it.

"Are you sure?" she asked.

"Positive," he assured her, slipping the credit card into the palm of her hand.

Ella almost jumped from the bolt of sexual tension that traveled from his hand to hers and raced along every nerve ending in her body. Her eyes widened in amazement that a simple touch could transfer such an intensity of emotion. A whimper escaped her lips as Hawk reached out with his other hand to steady her by the elbow. It had quite the opposite effect upon her. Her knees turned suddenly gelatinous.

"And I don't want you shopping the discount stores either," he told her sternly.

Ella hadn't the heart to tell him that Lander had few if

any exclusive shops. The thought of how Frannie would react to the discovery caused Ella to smile. Frannie could, of course, drive a hundred and fifty miles to Casper, an impractical endeavor given the time of day. Ella thought it also highly improbable that Frannie would ever leave Hawk and his nanny unsupervised overnight without the children to put a damper on any illicit happenings. The very thought coaxed a throaty laugh from Ella's throat.

"And I don't want you coming home until you can't stuff any more packages into the car either," he told her.

The look of incredibility upon Ella's face touched something deep inside Hawk. Having been married to a woman who demanded the finest of everything without regard to cost or an appreciative thank-you, he was surprised by how much he wanted to spoil Ella. He suddenly wanted nothing more than to accompany her into town where he could shower her with the kind of expensive shopping trip that would make her feel like a queen. Unfortunately, he'd already told Frannie that he was awaiting an important conference call, and he couldn't chance running into her and the children while shopping. In a town the size of Lander, the chances of avoiding one another were highly unlikely.

Not having had so much as a nibble for quite some time, Sarah threw down her pole and marched over to the picnic basket. "I'm hungry!" she complained.

"Me, too," Hawk growled in a low tone as he looked directly into Ella's eyes so that she could not mistake his innuendo.

Her stomach fluttered at his intended meaning, and she grew slick with wanting him. "Then let me feed you," she replied breathlessly.

Ella knew that both his body and soul were in need of nourishment. She had missed him something awful over the last couple of days and longed to reconnect in the most intimate of ways. That being impossible given their circumstances, she proceeded to satisfy his physical appetite, if not his carnal one.

He lay upon the blanket looking up at the clouds as if seeing them for the first time since his childhood. Beneath his adult burdens, he had almost forgotten how intense the sky was, how billowy the clouds.

When Hawk took his shoes off and dangled his toes over the bank, the children shouted their astonishment that their staid daddy found pleasure in the same simple things that so delighted their young hearts. They chomped happily upon celery sticks filled with peanut butter and raisins, a concoction Ella dubbed ants on a log, while she proceeded to put Hawk's head in her lap and feed him grapes one by one. The fact that it reminded them both of silly old movies featuring Roman slave girls and hedonistic rulers made the experience no less sensual. How long, she asked him, had it been since Hawk had played "pretend"?

Hawk couldn't remember exactly. He knew only that something about Ella put him in touch with a creative side that he had bound and gagged for the better part of his adult life. It wasn't so much that he was ready to abandon his charts and figures for good, just that maybe it was time to put them in their proper place in a life too encumbered by responsibilities.

"Yoo-hoo!" called an irritated voice from afar.

Frannie was waving her arms trying to get their attention. Her shopping attire looked slightly ridiculous from atop the adjacent hillside. Having so recently ruined her own under similar conditions, Ella could attest to the fact that high heels didn't hold up well beneath the punishment of rocky terrain. Her matching purse and hat would provide little cushioning if she tripped and came tumbling down the slope in a blaze of peach silk.

"Time to go, kids!" Frannie called, from her rocky roost above. Ella felt the woman's eagle eyes boring into her.

"We'll be right there," Hawk hollered in reply. A deep sigh insinuated just how disinclined he was to leave this peaceful sanctuary. He trailed the edge of his hand along the curve of her face and left his trademark tingle upon her skin. "We need to talk soon," he told Ella, reluctantly getting to his feet.

She couldn't have agreed more as she put her hand in his and allowed him to pull her up beside him. Together they gathered up fishing poles, uneaten lunches and any remaining trash. Billy refused to let go of his catch as he made his way up the hill with his drying trophy in hand. He was the first to reach the top.

"Look!" he exclaimed proudly, thrusting the fish in Frannie's face. "I caught it all by myself."

To her credit Frannie didn't scream or reprimand Billy for his social faux pas. "That's nice, dear," she managed to say without toppling from the boulder upon which she was sitting so daintily. "Maybe Ella can put it in the freezer so you can show it to all your friends."

"Or maybe I'll just cook it up with the ones I caught, and we can have a scrumptious down-home meal for supper tomorrow," she said, climbing up the steep slope with Hawk at her heels.

"Yummy!" decreed Sarah who was saving energy by riding piggyback on her daddy.

Frannie gave Ella a look intended to kill on sight. Clearly she preferred eating raw fish sushi-style to one that Ella had prepared in any countrified manner. Then again their fashionable guest was not used to eating "supper" period. Frannie had already chided her for using such gauche terminology. Apparently the rich ate "dinner." Not that Ella could see why it mattered anyway. As far as she could tell, Frannie maintained that chic skeletal figure by nibbling on little but crackers and rice cakes throughout the day.

When Hawk reached the top of the hill, huffing a little from his added load, Frannie launched herself from her boulder to hang on to his arm. For a moment Ella feared he might topple beneath all that feminine attention. Ever the gentleman, he set Sarah down and guided Frannie back down the rugged trail to the ranch house, which Ella noted she'd had no trouble maneuvering on her own getting there. Realizing it did her little good to brood over the way the two of them looked so fine together—Frannie so elegant and fragile-looking hanging on his arm and Hawk so deliciously virile—Ella turned her thoughts down a more productive avenue.

The anticipation of a shopping spree for herself was almost more than she could imagine. It was far too delectable an event to savor alone. Phoebe had wonderful taste in clothes and had often chided her friend for not sprucing up more often.

"Girl, with your figure if you'd give half an interest to what you're wearing, you'd have all the eligible bachelors in the country eating out of your talented little hand."

Bolstered by the thought that Phoebe might actually be able to help her find something that wouldn't embarrass Hawk at what was certain to be the social event of the year, she trudged back to the house unassisted with a smile on her face.

An hour and half later, she and Phoebe were combing the local hot spots for the latest in ballroom attire. Her friend threw a fit when Ella suggested rummaging through close-out racks of last season's prom dresses.

"Honey, when a man gives you his credit card and says to pick out something extra special, he isn't expecting you to show up in something from the clearance rack." Phoebe twirled a lock of her long, blond hair around her index finger in an uncharacteristically nervous mannerism.

"Are you sure I'm invited?" she asked.

"For the tenth time, I told you Her Highness requested I bring along some interesting artist types to add a certain avant-garde element to what is certain to be a lot of boring business types, and I can't think of anyone who could do that better than you."

Mentally Ella made a note to send Phoebe one of Frannie's fancy engraved invitations to allay any fears she may have about crashing the party.

"I have a hunch she was thinking more of Lyle Fenmore than Phoebe Tyler," Phoebe replied, tossing out the name of one of the state's most renowned artists.

Ultimately, the possibility of connecting with some fabulous man of means overcame any indecision on her part as she guided Ella toward their best bet in town, the bridal store. "With any luck, Shirley's got some dresses that don't look like taffeta bridesmaid cutouts."

Shirley assured them that she did indeed. In fact, she just had a shipment arrive earlier in the day that she was just in the process of hanging out. Buying something for Phoebe was a cinch. Her waist-length blond hair and svelte figure cried out for classic black satin with a thigh-high cut up one long leg. Ella was self-conscious about making her selection. Color was particularly important. She worried that her auburn hair would clash with any of the more vivid gowns with which Shirley suggested. Although she had no intention of competing with Frannie at this fete, she could not get the image out of her mind of that outrageously priced, silver bugle-beaded dress that she had hung up in the guest room. Next to that slinky creation, Ella was sure she would look like a stuffed sausage in whatever gown she chose.

Shirley and Phoebe both protested that the last thing she should do was cover up her fabulous hourglass figure. After much deliberation, Ella decided to trust her own instincts and chose a romantic country-style gown that suited her personality. Spaghetti straps held up an antique lace neckline and a matching hem peeked seductively out from a soft rayon crepe. The pearl buttons that ran up both sides accentuated her figure, and an unpretentious dark green bouquet print made a feminine understatement against which all the glitter in the world would have trouble competing. Though sedate on the hanger, the way Ella filled it out was most certainly not.

Not that anyone could convince her of how mouth-wateringly gorgeous she actually looked in the dress. As much as she would have loved to indulge in a daring little red-sequined number with a plunging neckline, Ella knew she would never feel comfortable in it. She was simply relieved to have found something that would neither embarrass her nor try to make her into something she was not.

She supposed her insecurity stemmed from her first junior high dance so long, long ago. Being an orphan, Ella hadn't the luxury of running out and buying trendy brand-name dresses off the rack. Instead, she used what little money she had saved and sewed her own party dress. So long had she labored over that dress, ripping out the seams and restitching until it was the absolute best she could make it, that Ella could still recall the fabric.

The color of lemon sherbet, the straight shift was offset

with a darling front panel of white eyelet and a short flared skirt. She had felt very grown up and almost pretty in it until she overhead a couple of the more popular girls making loud and cruel comments about ''Carrottop'' in her homemade frock. Ella pretended not to hear, and for the rest of the evening kept her chin bravely up, refusing to plant herself against the wall like so many of her peers. Feigning a boldness she did not feel, she coaxed more than one shy wallflower onto the dance floor and pretended to have a good time. Not until she was safely back in the dank basement room of her foster home did she allow her tears to fall freely.

With a car full of beautiful clothes, Ella hoped those ugly duckling days were behind her. However, she harbored no delusions about suddenly turning into a beautiful swan any time soon. Simply not tripping over her own two feet in front of Hawk's assemblage of esteemed guests would be enough for Ella to count the evening a success.

As silly as it was, Ella couldn't help but get lost in a fantasy in which her lovely new dress would magically transform her into a princess and cause Hawk to look at her with new eyes. What she really feared was that she would feel as homespun and out of place as she did back in junior high school when she'd been forced to endure the slings of snotty rich schoolgirls mocking her homemade clothes.

In between his obligations to his guests and pandering to Frannie's needs, Ella hoped Hawk would be able to fit in a dance or two with her. The thought of being held tightly in his arms and publicly acknowledged as a woman in her own right would be heavenly indeed. Unfortunately, her sense of joyful expectation was short-lived as anger and guilt dueled within her breast. Considering that Hawk certainly hadn't had any trouble dancing with her horizontally, she indignantly thought the least he could do was indulge her in a vertical waltz.

What a mess she had made of her life! Since she didn't have a mother to do it for her, Ella berated herself for falling too easily into bed with a man who was so far out of her reach. It was almost as stupid as falling hopelessly in love with him.

Twelve

Frannie was duly appalled at the lack of variety on her shopping foray into small-town America. As Ella had predicted, their persnickety visitor found nothing in Lander or nearby Riverton properly suitable, by which she meant extravagantly exclusive, for her niece's and nephew's grand entrance into society. Ella was tempted to tell her that "coming out" in Wyoming generally meant donning insulated boots when the year's first snow flew, but she doubted Frannie would appreciate her rustic sense of humor. The very thought of driving two hundred miles to the nearest mall in Casper was enough to make the poor woman very nearly choke on her morning toast.

"You've got to be kidding!"

"I'm sure the thought of traveling such a distance with little but sagebrush between here and there is daunting to a city girl such as yourself," Hawk replied sympathetically. "If I didn't have to fly back to Chicago to personally hammer out a persistent problem that unfortunately requires my immediate attention, I would be glad to drive you there myself.''

Frannie blanched. Ella wondered if it was from the thought of having to spend time alone with her and the children, but Hawk put his finger on the real reason.

''I promise to be back in time for the big bash,'' he assured her. He then took a moment to express his gratitude that he had been blessed with two such trustworthy adults with whom to leave his children while he attended to business. After his initial experience in single parenting, it wasn't something he was likely to take for granted ever again.

Somewhat mollified by his sincere appreciation, Frannie volunteered to drop Hawk off at the airport on her way out of town. Ella was relieved that her presence was not requested on this shopping expedition, one she anticipated would reach epic proportions and necessitate at least one night's accommodations at some ritzy hotel. Honestly, the thought of being alone for a couple of days without having to take care of anyone but herself sounded quite heavenly. She could certainly use the time to catch up on her own projects and possibly even get up the courage to submit her latest story to a publisher. Working with the children had indeed spurred her imagination, and she felt good about her most recent project. Not that one more rejection in a lifetime of them would likely kill her.

An added benefit of everyone being gone at the same time was that it would give Ella time to have her hair professionally cut and styled in time for the big do. The salary Hawk was paying her certainly afforded her such a common luxury. Not to mention that the excuse of a party in which she secretly hoped to wow the man was all the reason she really needed to splurge a little. She

knew that Phoebe, who so often chided her friend on her
ascetic attitude, would be proud of her for taking such
measures to advance her cause with the man she loved.

Luckily, as much as she personally disliked Frannie,
Ella wasn't worried about the children's welfare while in
her care. As far as she could tell, their aunt's affection for
them was as genuine as her feelings for Hawk. In an atmosphere where somebody else was being paid to cater to
Frannie's every whim, Ella was certain that they would
all have great fun together. Though Billy was sure to enjoy the hotel's swimming pool more than the shopping
expedition, she knew he would go along with whatever
his aunt requested of him if only to please her.

What Ella herself would have given to have had such
a colorful fairy godmother-type relative as a child! She
wouldn't dare interfere with the very special bond Billy
and Sarah had with their aunt, particularly given the fact
that they had lost their mother and this woman was one
of the few remaining links to her memory.

So it was that Ella found herself more resentful of
Hawk's leaving than of Frannie's imminent departure. It
would have been altogether obvious to anyone except
Hawk himself that his sister-in-law was doing everything
in her power to keep him so busy loading the car that he
didn't have a chance to say his private goodbyes to Ella.
When he was done, Frannie ushered him pell-mell out the
door. Ella barely had time to bid the children farewell
before the door shut behind them. Hearing Hawk's BMW
sports car start up made Ella feel interminably melan-
choly.

Wouldn't he have made up some excuse to see her
alone before leaving if she meant anything at all to him?

How very quiet it suddenly was with nothing but the
sound of her lonely heartbeat and the ticking of the grand-

father clock against the wall to fill the silence. Used to living in solitude for so much of her life, Ella was surprised how, without warning, it unnerved her. Sinking into the custom-made leather couch in the living room, she hugged a pillow to her chest and allowed herself a rare moment of self-pity.

"I miss you already."

The sound of that voice was unmistakable as it settled over Ella like a net from which she sought no escape. She snapped her head up to see Hawk standing in the living room door. Ella doubted whether even the pillow clutched over her heart could stifle the pounding rhythm of its beat. Hawk looked so strong and invincible leaning against the doorjamb that it evoked images of Hercules holding up the temple walls. It was all she could do to refrain from launching herself into his arms like the fool she was.

Surely those walls would crumble around them if she dared.

"I've *been* missing you," Ella pointedly replied.

She was, of course, referring to the fact that they had barely had a single moment together since Frannie had landed in the middle of Hawk's home like a human tornado. Giving voice to that resentment made Ella somehow sound more composed than she really felt.

"You didn't think I'd leave without saying goodbye, did you?"

A couple of long strides ate up the distance between them. Ella was on her feet and in Hawk's arms before either of them knew what hit them. His lips were a crushing force that reclaimed that which he took as his own. As starved for her touch as she for his, he ran his fingers through her hair and murmured soft words into their tangled tresses. Hawk held her like he never wanted to let her go, and she clung to him as if letting go would be a flagrant act of self-destruction. Wanting her to know exactly what effect she had upon him, he allowed his hands to travel the length of her body, cupping her rounded bottom and pulling her to him.

Ella groaned. She had worried that he had somehow managed to forget her. Proof otherwise lay in the depths of a pair of dove-gray eyes in which the flame of desire burned away remaining clouds of doubt. Ella may not have his heart unto herself, but at the moment she was certain that she had all of his very masculine attention.

"I don't want to leave," he told her.

"Then don't go."

Hawk moaned. "Don't tempt me."

He emphasized the plea by pulling her even closer to him. The sound of that deep voice applied so softly to her heart rumbled inside Ella, playing her like a native drum stretched ever so tautly. What a savage beat it struck inside her soul! That his strength was tempered by gentleness made Ella want to do something quite foreign to her nature. It made her want to throw her hard-fought independence to the wind and rely on him forever.

The noise of persistent honking outside caused Ella to jump in Hawk's arms. He swore softly under his breath. Ella had no doubt who was responsible for such rude behavior. Frannie could blame it on the children's impatience all she wanted, but Ella knew exactly what that woman was up to. In fact, the only thing that surprised her at all was that Frannie had allowed Hawk back into the house without trailing a half a step behind him.

Hawk kissed her goodbye and left her with a sad, haunting smile. Just a moment ago he had ravaged her mouth as if plundering her very soul. This parting kiss was its exact opposite. So tender was this meeting of lips that Ella almost wondered if she had imagined it. A butterfly lights no less gently than this kiss which settled so briefly upon her lips. Ella felt Hawk's breath enter her body and imagined this was the way Eve felt when first given life.

When Ella opened her eyes, he was gone. She felt incomplete, as if he had taken the best part of her with him. Running the tip of her index finger across her lips, she spoke to the spirit that he had left behind.

"I love you...."

The sound of her whisper echoing off the walls of the empty house was so disturbing that she reached for the one thing that never failed to give her comfort in her aloneness: her painting. Ella turned on some soothing music and allowed it to flow over and into her as she set her easel upon the deck. By the time the light was draining out of the sky and pooling in glorious colors along the horizon, she felt rejuvenated. Putting a hand to the middle of her back, she stretched her muscles.

Upon her easel sat a powerful painting that actually took her by surprise. In the act of immersing herself in the creative process, she had lost herself for the better part of the afternoon, leaving her looking at her own work as if it had been wrought by someone else entirely. It was a definite departure from her more whimsical renderings, this portrait of her lover in which his body was merged with that of a magnificent bird of prey, his namesake the red-tailed hawk. In a manner reminiscent of the crucifixion, a man's strong arms held the bird's wings aloft. Wounds inflicted by predators scarred his magnificent body glistening with sweat. The painting had such a potent effect upon the beholder that one was tempted to step away from the painting for fear of being seized by those massive claws and swept far, far away by a wingspan that covered the entire canvas.

Upon closer inspection, the creature's haunting eyes drew near the onlooker. They were as gray-blue as the sky holding him aloft and so piercing that one could almost believe they could see what was hidden within one's heart. There was also something vulnerable glistening in them that elicited a desire to embrace this creature and fly off with him to a more spiritual plane. Somehow Ella had managed to capture the man, the beast and his soul on canvas.

It was the most sensual piece of work she had ever created. Ella longed to touch her lips to those still wet from the finishing touches of her paintbrush. So pleased was she by the result of her efforts that she celebrated by pouring herself a glass of wine and enjoying the lingering light of sunset in the silent company of her masterwork. It was, she decided, far too special to be subjected to other's eyes just yet. Experience taught her that she was not a particularly objective judge of her own work, especially so soon upon completion. Nor did she want to chance Hawk seeing himself through her eyes. It would give him far too much power over her.

Frannie was sure to realize that a woman in love had painted this picture. Recognizing the passion in her strokes, she would likely offer to buy it—regardless of price. Ella smiled as she carefully took the painting off its easel. There wasn't enough money in the world to make her part with this particular portrait. It was going where she was heading in hopes of feeling less alone for the night: hung safe and sound above her old feather bed where the lingering smells and visual reminders of the man were less likely to rob her of any sleep than in his own home.

Frannie returned from Casper late the following day loaded down with packages and eager to get started on her plans for the upcoming party. For once she seemed more than happy to let Ella take care of the children while she focused her considerable energy into tormenting the florist, the caterer, the cleaning staff, the valets, the waiters and the musicians, all of whom she'd hired for the party scheduled for the coming Saturday night. When Hawk called to say that he would be detained for a couple of days, she pursed her lips in consternation then sighed with relief at his renewed promise to be back by the end of the week.

Frannie was so busy making arrangements that she scarcely had time to demand that Ella cater to her special needs twenty-four hours a day. Ella was glad to cut the woman wide berth in Hawk's absence. A virtual whirlwind of activity, Frannie was definitely in her element as a social director. Ella couldn't help but admire her organizational abilities and notice the spot of color in her pale cheeks placed there by her excitement at the task at hand. It went through her mind that a man of Hawk's standing was truly better suited to a woman like Frannie who knew how to advance him socially rather than someone like her who was just glad to be left alone to tend to the children and enjoy her own fertile imagination.

Indeed, swimming and fishing down in the quiet pools by the apple trees was far more to her liking. Ella was far more comfortable with a worn storybook, her art supplies and a picnic basket full of finger foods than she could ever be planning some stuffy coterie. The more Frannie fluttered around making a big deal out of the tiniest details, the more uncomfortable Ella became with the idea of putting in an appearance at the party herself. The last thing she wanted to do was embarrass herself—or, God forbid, Hawk—at a function that was clearly so important to his standing in the community. Indeed, having grown up in the area, Ella full well knew how much some people set store in the political and historical ties of its residents. As much as it helped, money alone couldn't buy one's way into the inner circle of the town's gentry.

What had initially sounded like such fun was starting to sound like a trial by fire. Ella figured if she could just make an appearance in her beautiful new dress, impress Hawk with her sudden savoir faire, and sneak in a couple of dances with him without making any terrible social transgressions in conversing with some ambassador or another, she would count the night a success. She was glad Phoebe would be there to offer her support. Hopefully Frannie wouldn't have a conniption fit when the gorgeous blonde arrived and presented the gilded invitation Ella had sneaked out of the stack and mailed herself. With myriad guests invited, she hoped Frannie wouldn't notice one way or the other. Not that Phoebe was one to fade into the woodwork. Ella knew for a fact that her dear friend was pinning her hopes on finding a suitably rich, handsome man for herself at this shindig.

When the big day arrived at last with no sign of Hawk by early afternoon, Frannie grew frantic. Obviously this party was far more to her than a simple housewarming celebration. It seemed to encompass her expectations in the most tangible of ways. Wisely, everyone stayed out of Frannie's way. Maintaining that they would need all their energy for the party, Ella put Billy and Sarah down for a long nap before proceeding to try something different with her hair. The beautician's cut made it lay nice about her shoulders and shaped it around her face in a flattering style, but for tonight, Ella wanted something that made her look less like the girl next door and more like the mature woman she was.

Wrinkling her nose at the freckles she saw reflected in the mirror, she pulled her thick mane of hair up and away from her face. The hairdresser had showed her how to fashion a sophisticated upswept style. She also sold Ella a fake pearl-encrusted comb that took only a little expertise to master. When Ella was done, she pulled a few stray locks from confinement and fashioned a half dozen romantic ringlets about her face. She hoped the effect would be more dramatic once she changed out of her bibbed jean overalls and white T-shirt.

She took her dress out of the closet and gently tore away the paper wrapper that protected it. Holding her breath as if worried that the gown had somehow lost its appeal since she had first tried it on, Ella broke into a smile to rediscover the loveliest article of clothing she had ever owned. She dressed carefully, taking her time in fastening every single pearl button along the sides of the garment. The deep green print accentuated the color of her eyes, and the lace flounce added just the right romantic element to what might otherwise be a rather unassuming dress.

Ella lightly dusted her freckles with powder in hopes of making them disappear, tried lengthening her eyelashes with mascara and artfully applied a frosted pink lipstick the color of cotton candy. When she finished, Ella twirled around in front of her full-length mirror like she might have as a child had anyone ever bought her such pretty clothes for the birthday parties to which she wasn't invited.

She stared at herself for a moment as if looking at a stranger. Why, she actually looked pretty! The figure she had always considered too rounded did not at all look plump in the folds of a dress designed to show off a woman's natural curves. Ella's green eyes were aglow with excitement. Her gown may not be the most expensive or trendy at the party, but it certainly did flatter her. Indeed, it was a far cry from the outfit she'd worn the first day she had met Hawk. In fact, with the clothes she'd bought at his insistence, she'd relegated that faded, old garment to the trash bin.

A spot of perfume at her wrists and she was ready to face the world. She woke the children and bid them don their own party clothes. Sarah could barely contain her excitement, but Billy balked. Ella could see why once she got a good look at the outfit his aunt had picked out for him. He looked rather like Little Lord Fauntleroy in his blue velvet britches with a white lace hanky poking out of his pocket. It matched Sarah's dress, and truly the two of them made an adorable picture. Nonetheless, poor Billy feared he would have to fight every boy in the vicinity once they got a gander at what he classified as "sissy clothes." Though Ella suspected he was right, she wasn't about to broach the subject with his aunt. Not when she was already so riled up about how late Hawk was.

The opening of the front door brought a sigh of relief to everyone who heard it. It seemed Hawk was home at last.

"Daddy!" cried the children, vaulting out of their respective rooms and burnishing the banister with the seats of their matching velvet togs.

Ella followed. Standing at the top of the grand stairway, she watched Hawk embrace his children. He hugged them as if he hadn't seen them for years and tossed them into the air to make them squeal in delight. The sight made Ella's heart swell and her eyes grow misty. Surely, this man who had given up so much by moving here for his children had gained more than the world could count in gold coins locked in any of its vaults. She wondered if his wife had appreciated the treasure she had in the father of their children and felt sorry that the dead woman was missing out on such beautiful sights.

Hawk looked up and saw Ella standing above him, an angelic vision in pearls and lace if ever he'd seen one. It was one of those moments that freeze time and immortalize a glance. Ella watched his eyes widen in surprise and felt a rush of warmth washing through her limbs at the realization that he did indeed like what he saw. The initial weariness that she spied in him when he walked through the door was replaced by undeniable masculine appreciation. Feeling like Scarlett O'Hara poised so at the top of the stairs, Ella bid her strappy stiletto heels remain rooted to their spot. It would not do to tumble down the stairs and ruin the effect she had waited a lifetime to achieve.

"You look stunning," he told her simply.

For once in her life, Ella believed him. His words brought a smile to her face that warmed their singular part of the universe. Feeling certain that losing that smile would be akin to shutting off the sun, Hawk held out his hands to her. Ella fought the urge to fly into his arms in the same unrestrained manner with which his children had greeted him. After a lifetime of anguish and loneliness, this all seemed too wonderful to be real. Twilight cast a glow upon the scene, heightened by the effect of hundreds of twinkling lights strung throughout the entire lower floor. The magnificent house seemed to Ella a fairy kingdom perfumed by the bowers of fresh flowers.

Ella stood quite still and took the view in sweet, deep breaths. She took a long moment to study Hawk's face and found it every bit as handsome as she remembered it. Her gaze fell upon his suit pocket where she discerned a bulge the exact size and shape of a ring box. Green eyes flew open in surprise. Her breath caught in her lungs, and she momentarily forgot to breathe, necessitating the need to grab hold of the banister for support lest she pass out on the spot. She hastened to tell herself that she could be mistaken. For all she knew, he could be carrying the latest in microchips in that breast pocket. It wouldn't do to get all excited over a mistaken assumption.

The children were oblivious to the sexual awareness in the look shared between the two adults poised so prettily at the top and the bottom of the great stairway. Another set of eyes was not, however. Hearing the front door open, Frannie had hurried into the entryway. What she saw froze the blood in her veins and gave her pause to watch a long moment in the shadows before making her presence known.

"Hawk, darling!" she said at last, breaking the magical spell with a forced smile.

Embracing her brother-in-law, Frannie kissed him on both cheeks before chiding him for arriving just "in the nick of time." Glancing at the diamond-studded watch on her wrist, she bid him hurry and put on his tux before the first of their guests arrived.

"Children," she said in a velvet voice that broached no discussion, "go wait on the deck. Help yourself to some canapés, but don't make yourself sick and please don't spill on your lovely outfits. I've hired someone to take our family portrait, and I don't want you getting dirty before the night is immortalized."

Their "Yes, ma'am," was prompt and courteous as they hurried from the room.

"Just a minute. I'd like to have a word with you," Frannie called as Ella started down the stairs to accompany the children. She knew full well that her duties toward the children remained the same, party or no.

Frannie waited to make sure the door to Hawk's bedroom was closed before gliding to the top of the stairs herself. She seemed to glitter in that stunning silver-beaded dress that Ella had imagined she would wear. Slit up the side, it revealed a length of one thin, shapely leg. Her hair matched her gown in a shimmering waterfall of light, cut in a chic blunt style.

Next to her, Ella felt like a country bumpkin and suddenly she was back to that first awful junior high dance when all it took to reduce her from a princess to a toad was a couple of well-aimed slurs. She fought the urge to curtsey as Frannie ran her pale blue eyes up and down the length of her.

"My dear, I'm afraid there has been a terrible mistake."

Ella felt the blood in her veins drop several degrees. The woman's words might be civil, but the look in those narrowed eyes was anything but genteel.

"I'm guessing that by your charming *getup* that you were under the impression that you were actually expected to attend this party. I am sorry. I thought it was understood that you would be minding the children and staying out of the way as much as possible."

"I'd be glad to do that," Ella assured her over the sinking feeling of disappointment. The look on Hawk's face when he saw her a moment ago would be enough to sustain her for a lifetime—with or without the dance she had so longed to share with him.

Unappeased by the promise, Frannie chose her words as carefully as a cat plucks unsuspecting birds from the air. "My dear child, I saw the way that you looked at Hawk a moment ago. That love-struck look written all over your face makes me feel terribly guilty that I didn't confide in you sooner. You see, if I'd realized your feelings earlier, I could have possibly spared you some pain."

"What are you talking about?" Ella asked. She had no desire to be anything other than direct. Word games were not her style any more than glittering evening gowns that cost more than comprehensive medical care for many small villages.

"I hate to break it to you this way, but you need to understand this is more than simply a housewarming party. It's a surprise engagement party."

Ella looked at her stupidly, and Frannie was forced to explain more precisely.

"My dear girl, Hawk and I are going to be married."

Thirteen

"**C**ongratulations," Ella stammered.

The words echoed in her head as if she were hearing them from some hollow place far, far away. Some place like her heart.

So she hadn't been wrong about that bulge in Hawk's pocket being a ring box after all. She'd just screwed up the part about the intended recipient of that engagement ring. Ella didn't need to berate herself for being such a silly fool to ever entertain fantasies about a man like Hawk proposing on bended knee to someone of her lowly social stature. After all, she had Frannie to drive that point home with the tip of a poisoned sword.

"I can tell by the look on your face that this comes as quite a surprise to you. Anyone can see that you're clearly enamored of Hawk, and while I can't say as I blame you, neither can I believe that you actually thought for even a

second that anything could ever come of your brash flir-
tation but heartache."

Ella bit her lip to keep from crying. *Why the hell not?*
she wanted to demand. *Why is it so inconceivable that
Hawk could fall in love with me?* Instead she merely nodded her head, hoping her mute agreement would be
enough to make Hawk's beautiful fiancée shut up and stop
tormenting her.

"I don't want to hurt you, Ella, really I don't."

For an instant her Siamese blue eyes softened just
enough that Ella could almost believe her.

Frannie even had the aplomb to look sorry for what she
was about to do. She took a deep breath and reminded
herself that undermining one so obviously unaware of her
natural beauty was part of that old adage about all being
fair in love and war.

"Surely you must understand that a man like Hawk
needs someone of a similar social standing to be at his
side, not just raising his children, but also advancing him
politically and financially. Someone who is a match for
him intellectually and culturally. God knows, I better than
anyone else understand how hard it will be to fill Lauren's
shoes, but let me assure you no one is better able than I
to do just that—both as a mother and as a wife. Hawk
and I share more than just a history together. We have a
similar understanding of how the world works. As much
as you'd like to believe otherwise, it is not made up of
fairy godmothers and happily-ever-after endings in which
one goes from rags to riches, from poverty to instant acceptance by the upper echelon. I hate to be the one to
burst your bubble, Ella, but this is not some Cinderella
Ranch where a lowly nanny's fantasies come true just by
wishing it were so."

Wounded to be spoken to like some idiotic schoolgirl

with nothing more than a passing crush, Ella studied Frannie standing there as cool as the drink she held in her hand. The woman's beauty was not marred by her ruthlessness. Ella wondered if she ought to set the record straight and let this haughty diva know that her betrothed had shared more than a longing look or two with her. Surely as his wife-to-be Frannie deserved to know of Hawk's penchant for finger painting in the nude.

As tempting as it was to strike back in retaliation for the slurs Frannie had heaped upon her, Ella didn't have it in her to be so cruel. As quickly at the idea entered her mind, it was offset by the realization that Frannie hadn't so much as been on the scene before she and Hawk had consummated their passion. It wasn't exactly like he'd been cheating on Frannie with her. Nor had Hawk ever given her any indication that he wished to advance their relationship beyond the one-time fling which she had so shamelessly initiated. He most certainly had never alluded to marriage. In fact, in avoiding any mention of his dead wife, he had given the impression that he would never marry again.

Apparently it had just taken the right woman to change his mind. Another, more beautiful woman who looked and acted like his beloved Lauren.

Clutching her hand over her shattered heart, she didn't know what good it would do to hurt Frannie. In the world of the rich and famous, Ella supposed sexual dalliances were accepted, if not politely condoned, as part of some ritualistic game between a jaded set of men and women.

Ella flinched when Frannie laid a gentle hand upon her bowed shoulder.

"I hope you understand what an awkward position this puts us all in. Me, especially. And you, as well. Clearly Hawk appreciates you for bailing him out during his time of need, and the children are obviously quite fond of you. Still in all, I just don't think it's appropriate to encourage a young woman so smitten with my fiancé to remain in our employ, do you?''

Ella most certainly did not. The thought of working in Hawk's house as his wife's personal servant was more than Ella could bear to imagine. Not to mention how intolerable it would be to have him so near each day and not be able to touch him. Not be able to share her true feelings with him. If there was such a thing as hell on earth, Ella was sure that would have to fit the description.

Tears that she refused to allow Frannie to see clogged her throat. Unable to speak, Ella emphatically shook her head no. Indeed not only wouldn't it be good for the newlyweds to have her underfoot, it most definitely wouldn't be fair to her.

''Good, I'm glad we have an understanding on just why your services are no longer needed. Not that I want you to worry about money. I'll see that you get a year's severance pay.''

Ella couldn't bring herself to thank the woman for what appeared on the surface to be a more than generous offer. She supposed in Frannie's world money was used to solve every problem and salve every conscience. What a pity Ella's heart couldn't be so easily pieced back together with currency.

''Considering how painful this is for both of us, I think it best if your termination is effective immediately. That way you won't have to subject yourself to the public announcement of our marriage and Hawk won't be distracted by your...'' She almost said ''beauty'' but caught herself. ''Presence.''

Donning a most sympathetic expression Frannie asked,

"Will you trust me to explain to Hawk the reasons for your leaving?"

Ella couldn't blame her for not wanting their nanny's mental breakdown to ruin her big moment and was, in fact, grateful not to have to face Hawk herself.

Ever again if she could help it.

"I'd appreciate that," she managed to choke out before fleeing down the stairs and out the front door into the night.

Hawk saw but a flash of dark green floral print slipping past the valets and dodging the guests who were just beginning to arrive en mass. Recognizing the material of Ella's dress, he called after her to see what was the matter. Rather than stopping at the sound of her name, she didn't so much as turn her head to glance in his direction. Instead, Ella tore down the driveway, avoiding oncoming traffic in her high heels before veering off toward the woods, a sprite who left but a wisp of lace behind.

Coming up behind him, Frannie placed a restraining hand upon Hawk's elbow. In a voice as sultry as the breeze that toyed with the silver beads of her dress, she cajoled him. "You mustn't be rude, darling. Your guests are sure to feel slighted if you run off before you've so much as met some of them."

The look on Hawk's face left little doubt that he didn't give a fig about social propriety at the moment. The determination in his eyes caused Frannie to expel a long-suffering sigh and simultaneously stamp one dainty foot upon the ground. "If you must know, the undependable little thing just up and gave notice that she was quitting. I'll be glad to give you the details later, but right now I'd appreciate it if you'd act civilly to all the gracious people I've invited to your home on your behalf. Whether you are aware of it or not, I've worked damned hard to pull this party together, and I will be terribly hurt if you abandon me to chase after the hired help.''

Hawk was just about to take umbrage with the term his sister-in-law used to describe the woman he loved when the governor stepped forward to introduce himself and his wife. An informal line quickly formed behind them, and Hawk drew a polite smile over the teeth he had to strain to keep from gritting.

"We will talk later," he informed the woman at his side.

Frannie flashed him a smile as dazzling as her designer dress and ran a hand over the jewelry box bulge in his tuxedo pocket. "I certainly hope so," she told him, her eyes filled with hope.

As the orchestra struck its first chord, Ella was fighting her way through the underbrush. It was all too reminiscent of the last time she'd traipsed through the woods with Hawk's children in tow. Her hair had come undone, and once again her shoes were ruined beyond repair. When a thornbush caught the lacy hem of her ankle-long skirt, Ella did not stop to save it, but rather tore onward leaving a scrap of the fancy frill behind.

Tears that she had proudly refused to let fall in Frannie's presence freely watered a trail lighted by naught but the moon overhead. As the sound of the music from the ranch grew fainter, she paused briefly to catch her breath. Pulling the faux pearl barrette from her hair, she tossed it into the thicket as far away as she possibly could throw it.

If only her memories could be so easily disposed of!

By the time she reached her darkened cabin, Ella was a mess. Mascara ran down her face, her dress was in shreds, and her hair hung loose about her face in a mass of tangles. Once safely inside, she lit the kerosene lantern and approached Hawk's portrait with her shattered love. Another scorned woman might have taken a knife to the painting and rent it in two like her heart, attempting to take her anger out on the image of the man who had hurt her so deeply. Standing before the portrait, Ella felt familiar waves of shame wash over her.

Why was it that she was never enough for someone to love? Memories of days gone by washed over her in a deluge of pain. Truly nothing had changed in her life since a childhood when no one wanted her beyond the services she could render. No amount of smiling agreeably and being helpful and trying her hardest to please could ever make anyone love a freckled-faced urchin whose own father hadn't wanted to claim her. Nothing had changed since that awful junior high dance when Ella had been so determined to pry open people's hearts with a bubbly personality and a genuine desire to make everyone feel important in his own right. No, nothing had changed—other than the names and the faces of those who looked down upon her and used her for their own personal gain.

Was it unfair to lump Hawk in that last category? Indeed Ella had given her love freely and expected nothing in return. Which is exactly what she got.

But was it what she deserved?

Ella liked to think not. She desperately wanted to hold on to the belief that any love, no matter how excruciating the toll it exacted, was better than spending a lifetime in which one was too afraid to trust another human being with one's frailties. She needed to believe that love tested one like gold under fire and, no matter the outcome, made one better for having risked while on this earth.

And so it was that, rather than wielding a knife to the

portrait of her lover, Ella brushed it tenderly with the back of one hand before sinking onto her old feather bed where she sobbed herself to sleep to the accompaniment of a coyote's lonely, lonely song.

Hawk was glad that Hissy Face had decided to accompany him on this jaunt into the neighboring wilderness. It was a long shot that the cat would actually remember its mistress's home, but Hissy had been insistent about coming along, weaving in and out of Hawk's legs and darn near tripping him with every step he took. It was almost as if the kitten knew that he needed her.

Having never been to Ella's home before, Hawk very nearly missed it. Tucked into the trees, the tiny cottage was easy to overlook. It was but the faintest glimmer of a candle flame that drew him down the seldom-traveled path that led to Ella's doorstep. Clutching a bit of lace in one hand and a flashlight in the other, Hawk could not bring himself to believe that this tumbledown shack was the magical cottage of which his children spoke in such glowing terms. He shone his flashlight over it. Surely this was just an outbuilding to house gardening tools and winter equipment in the off-seasons.

Hissy jumped up on the windowsill and proceeded to let out a long, plaintive wail. The cat's assurance that this was familiar territory gave Hawk reason to pause before passing the cabin by altogether. The dim flickering of a light inside beckoned to him. He raised his hand to the front door and brought it down with enough force to rattle the structure.

"Who is it?" came Ella's startled cry.

"It's me," Hawk called roughly not bothering with his name.

"Go away!"

He didn't bother arguing with her. Hawk placed his shoulder against the door and put all his weight behind it. Living as she did, Ella had never bothered with security locks, and the single bolt she used gave way as easily as she had given herself to Hawk. Wood splintered, and dust flew. Ella drew herself up in her bed with a homemade quilt clutched to her heart.

"What do you want?" she demanded to know.

Hawk didn't answer. He was too busy looking for a light switch. After stumbling around in the dark for a long moment, he came to realize that the cabin was without electricity. Using only the light from the kerosene lamp burning atop a rough-hewn table in the center of the room, he discovered that not only was there no electricity or phone, it appeared the only water available was from the old hand pump out front. He shook his head in disbelief. This couldn't possibly be where Ella had actually resided before coming to work for him.

Tears sprung to his eyes. He was ashamed that he'd ever thought this gentlewoman a gold digger. That she lived within such achingly modest means cracked his heart wide open like an egg. He'd had no idea.

No idea other than the way she looked at his home as if it were a castle or the way she never spent anything on herself or how she treated hot baths and central air as if they were untold luxuries. He rebuked himself for not reading the signs which had been posted all over the place had he but opened his eyes to see.

How Ella had managed to turn such squalid conditions into a homey environment with little more than some paint and an artistic flair was nothing short of amazing. Hawk had been too self-absorbed in his own problems to actually take her talent seriously. Studying the paintings that lined the walls, he realized what a mistake that had been. They defied his initial belief that her interest in art was simply the diversion it had been for so many of Lauren's bored women friends. The difference being that Ella's work showed genuine talent.

Though her fanciful depictions of Western gnomes and fairies hidden in the landscape appealed to the child in him, the man in him responded at a purely gut level to the most powerful rendition of a hawk that he had ever seen. Impossible not to recognize himself in the bold strokes, he was flattered by the way she had captured his masculine aura. If this was truly the way she saw him, Hawk knew he would be a fool to ever let her go.

Her pride already hurt, Ella stiffened her backbone against Hawk's opinion of her humble home, of her artistic ability, and of her, period. Unable to mention his upcoming wedding in any but an indirect manner, she glanced meaningfully at the gaping hole where her door used to be.

"If you're looking for a baby-sitter while you're on your honeymoon, I've got to tell you that you've come *knocking* on the wrong door."

Striking an indignant pose in her cotton pajamas put Ella at a decided disadvantage. Hawk, on the other hand, looked fabulous in a Western-cut black tuxedo. His white shirt fairly glowed in the dim light.

"I am afraid that I do need your help in that department if the wedding is going to go off as planned," he told her sheepishly. His presence swallowed up the small abode.

Ella couldn't believe he had the gall to speak to her thus. As always in times of greatest pain, Ella called upon a reserve of sorely wounded pride to hold her chin up high.

"Let me be among the first to congratulate you," she

said over the railroad tie stuck sideways in her throat. "But I'm afraid I'll be unavailable then."

That Hawk actually had the audacity to approach her four-poster bed and hazard to sit down beside her sent Ella scuttling as far away from him as the span of old bed would allow. Flattening herself against the rough log walls, she pulled the blanket up to her chin.

Hawk shook his head in disappointment. "That's going to put quite a damper in my plans," he said, reaching for her hands.

Ella swore she would slap him if he dared suggest that they remain "friends." She hadn't thought him capable of such thoughtless cruelty. As if stung by his touch, she pulled her hands out of his.

He looked hurt by her reaction. "You see," he explained, "my sister-in-law has volunteered to fill in the baby-sitter position. Now all I have to do is locate a willing bride for the ceremony."

Ella looked at him as if he had lost his mind. At last, understanding dawned in her features as she leapt to a terrible conclusion. From the horrified expression on his face when he first surveyed his surrounding, she assumed that he must see her as a charity case. Perhaps he was under the mistaken impression that she was pregnant and it was her crazy hormones that had driven her running out of his house into the night. And then there was the insidious possibility that Frannie might have turned him down, thus making Ella second choice in providing his children a stand-in mother. Whatever his reasoning, she hastened to set the man straight.

"You are under no obligation to propose out of pity for me," she told him stiffly. "That is, if you call what just transpired a proposal. Besides, I thought you and Frannie—''

"Are very dear friends," Hawk finished for her. "It seems Frannie thought I was capable of feeling something more for her, but when I assured her that it is you I love, she very graciously suggested I go after you."

Those sweet words had the power to resuscitate a heart Ella had thought dead just a few short hours ago. Hawk loved her! He had said the words aloud, hadn't he? Still, Ella couldn't quite believe her ears. Nor could she imagine Frannie feeling anything but contempt for her. Nonetheless she was struck by a sense of pity for the elegant woman who had everything that money could buy—except her heart's desire.

"Is she going to be all right?" Ella heard herself asking.

"I imagine that as we speak she and Phoebe are vying for the attention of every eligible bachelor at the party. By the way, your friend has a wicked tongue which she used to lash me soundly before shoving me out the door, promising to entertain my guests for the remainder of the evening, and pointing me in the general direction of your home."

Ella smiled at the image. She hoped Phoebe would someday find the Prince Charming she deserved. And where better than at an official fancy dress ball at what was destined to be the site of her best friend's wedding?

Ella jumped in surprise when Hissy Face joined them on the bed, demanding a share of the credit for bringing these two star-crossed lovers together. Taking the cat in her arms, she feigned a preoccupation with petting the precocious feline.

"You aren't just asking me to marry you because you need a charity to write off on your taxes?" she wanted to know. "Because I'll have you know I'm perfectly capable of taking care of myself. I have been for years."

With that, she took a letter from a ledge above the bed and thrust it at Hawk.

"It's from a publisher," she announced proudly.

The letter which had arrived earlier in the day provided little balm for Ella's broken heart. In the light of Hawk's proposal, it gave her a thread of self-reliance to cling to if this man were motivated by anything other than love.

"They want to buy one of my children's books. With the advance they've offered, I'll be able to start college full-time next semester."

Hawk didn't bother unfolding the letter though his smile alone would have provided enough illumination for him to read it comfortably. "That's wonderful," he told her, sounding genuinely happy with her success. "But there's no need for you to reiterate the fact that you can manage very well on your own with me, angel. I'm the one who desperately needs you."

That said, Hawk proceeded to get down upon one knee at her bedside and pull a ring box from his pocket. "Will you marry me, Ella?"

Ella took the velvet case into her hands and felt its warmth spill into her palms and spread into her heart. Taking a deep breath, she forced herself to tempt fate. If she were to accept his proposal, it had to be on her terms. She wanted the whole fairy tale, not simply the trappings.

"Only if you're not in the market for a substitute mother for your children. And a substitute wife for Lauren."

Hawk looked so startled by the idea that Ella had to believe his intentions pure. Her name was a sweet echo off the four walls that sheltered them.

"Ella, darling," he said. "There's something you need to know. I'm not sure exactly what you believe about my marriage, but the truth of the matter is that Lauren only

married me for my money because her family was in dire
financial straits.''

Hawk paused a long time not so much to let that startling bit of information sink in but because what he was
about to share was so painful that he had only recently
come to terms with it himself.

''Lauren was with her lover when she was in the accident that took her life.''

''Oh, Hawk,'' Ella exclaimed with a compassion that
superseded any reservations she ever might have had.

All the time she thought he was avoiding the subject
of Lauren hadn't been to preserve the sanctity of their
marriage vows but rather because it evoked such disturbing memories of her ultimate betrayal. How agonizing it
must have been for him to share his humiliation with her.

''Of course I'll never tell the children,'' he said gruffly.
''I don't know what good it would do to tarnish the memory of their mother that way. But I want you to know,
Ella, that you are twice the mother to them that Lauren
ever thought of being. And more of a woman than she
could have ever hoped to become.''

''I love you,'' Ella told him, thinking Lauren a fool.
''You, not your money or your status. You. And, yes, I
will marry you.''

With that, she bid him get up from the cold wooden
floor to join her beneath the covers of a bed warmed by
her body. What did it matter that the wind was whistling
in through the broken door when they could keep each
other sheltered from the cold world without? It was time
to prove to Hawk and to herself that hearts do their best
healing one beat at a time.

Declaring her life truly fairy-tale perfect, Ella embraced
the helpless, hopeless, hungry feeling of being in love
with the most wonderful man in the world. Kneeling pre-

cariously upon the old feather bed, Ella directed her fingers to the buttons of his tuxedo. A moment later she sent his jacket sailing across the room, quickly followed by shirt, tie, pants and briefs.

Once he was naked and hard and in her arms, she whispered, "There's only one thing left that worries me."

Hawk stiffened in her arms and she hastened to explain lest she worry him needlessly.

"I left the finger paints back at your place."

Hawk's laugh was half-growl. "Don't you worry," he said nibbling on the hollow of her neck in the very spot that made her wild. "I'm going to paint you all the colors of the world and give it back to you on a silver platter."

Ella sighed contentedly as he proceeded to do just that, brushing her from head to toe with his fingers and tongue and entire body. No mere canvas could hold the colors that exploded in Ella's mind as Hawk made love to her in such a deliberate fashion most women could but imagine in their sweetest dreams. Glorious pinks and golds of a summer sunrise, dazzling silver from stars sprinkling the heavens above, iridescent greens and blues of mermaids playing tag amid whitecaps, roses and rainbows and indigo twilights all were evoked by the gentleness of Hawk's touch.

That he was capable of such tenderness was Ella's undoing. None of the frantic haste which distinguished their earlier lovemaking marred the passion of their newly pronounced commitment to each another. Languid and deep flowed the river of their love. Hawk kissed the fragrant tresses of Ella's hair, her eyelids, her nose, down her neck, along the soft, sensitive underside of her arms, out to the palms of her work roughened hands to the sensitive nerves of her fingertips.

She begged him to stop and allow her to return his

kisses, but he bid her remain still and continued his erotic path over her full, sensitive breasts, savoring the taste of her nipples in his mouth. "So sweet," he murmured lovingly, making her ache with longing for him. No part of her body, nary a single rib, escaped the nips and nibbles that marked her tenderly as his own. Ella pulled that magnificent head of his up to her own and orchestrated the sounds of his slow, eager surrender.

Kissing him softly at first, she tasted the promise on his lips, then slowly deepened it in a deliberate attempt to physically share her very soul with him. The cat curled up at the foot of the bed purred no more contentedly than did Ella.

In the flickering light, the painting of that mystical bird which Ella had painted came to life. As it lifted its magnificent wings, Ella felt herself lifted higher and higher above the mundane world. Sprouting wings herself, she competed move for move with her partner in a crescendo of airborne acrobatics. Together they climbed the heavens toward the peak of ecstasy. Mesmerized by each other, they locked talons at the height of their passionate dance, and the two became one, spiritually and physically.

Plummeting through the sky in a death-defying free fall, they tumbled through the clouds past hundreds of feet of sheer cliff walls. Just before reaching the surface of a shimmering lake below, something purely magical happened. Feeling Ella tremble in his arms at the peak of passion, Hawk groaned aloud. Shuddering, he gave all of himself, spreading his wings wide and bidding her soar with him back toward the sun. Spent, they glided effortlessly above a world so far beneath them that it couldn't hope to ever touch what they felt for one another.

This sacred act of merging love and sensuality in no way diminished their need for touch. Not the kind of thoughtless lover to roll away once his more immediate needs were sated, Hawk planned on sustaining this intimacy for a lifetime. Declaring that Ella's fresh-eyed innocence had given him another chance at making a good life for his children—and himself—he held her tenderly in his arms and made plans for a future together.

A future that included laughter and children and magic. A future worthy of the kind of happily-ever-after that everyone deserves, but only the bravest of hearts is willing to commit a lifetime not only to make come true, but to last forever.

A once-upon-a-time skeptic, Ella allowed herself to accept the fairy tale ending that truly belonged to her. Circumstances of birth and lack of opportunity were nothing in comparison to how this wonderful man made her feel. No longer the ugly duckling of her youth, she was transformed into a real-life Cinderella and made beautiful, not by the twirling of a godmother's wand, but by the power of Hawk's eternal love.

*   *   *   *   *

THE FORTUNES OF TEXAS

invite you to meet

THE LOST HEIRS

Silhouette Desire's scintillating new miniseries, featuring the beloved

FORTUNES OF TEXAS

and six of your favorite authors.

A Most Desirable M.D.—June 2001
by Anne Marie Winston (SD #1371)

The Pregnant Heiress—July 2001
by Eileen Wilks (SD #1378)

Baby of Fortune—August 2001
by Shirley Rogers (SD #1384)

Fortune's Secret Daughter—September 2001
by Barbara McCauley (SD #1390)

Her Boss's Baby—October 2001
by Cathleen Galitz (SD #1396)

Did You Say Twins?!—December 2001
by Maureen Child (SD #1408)

And be sure to watch for *Gifts of Fortune*,
Silhouette's exciting new single title,
on sale November 2001

*Don't miss these unforgettable romances…
available at your favorite retail outlet.*

Silhouette®
Where love comes alive™

Visit Silhouette at www.eHarlequin.com   SDFOT

SILHOUETTE® MAKES YOU A STAR!

Feel like a star with Silhouette.

We will fly you and a guest to New York City for an exciting weekend stay at a glamorous 5-star hotel. Experience a refreshing day at one of New York's trendiest spas and have your photo taken by a professional. Plus, receive $1,000 U.S. spending money!

**Flowers…long walks…dinner for two…
how does Silhouette Books
make romance come alive for you?**

Send us a script, with 500 words or less, along with visuals (only drawings, magazine cutouts or photographs or combination thereof). Show us how Silhouette Makes Your Love Come Alive. Be creative and have fun. No purchase necessary. All entries must be clearly marked with your name, address and telephone number. All entries will become property of Silhouette and are not returnable. **Contest closes September 28, 2001.**

Please send your entry to: **Silhouette Makes You a Star!**

In U.S.A.
P.O. Box 9069
Buffalo, NY, 14269-9069

In Canada
P.O. Box 637
Fort Erie, ON, L2A 5X3

Look for contest details on the next page, by visiting www.eHarlequin.com or request a copy by sending a self-addressed envelope to the applicable address above. Contest open to Canadian and U.S. residents who are 18 or over. Void where prohibited.

Silhouette®
Where love comes alive™

Our lucky winner's photo will appear in a Silhouette ad. Join the fun!

SRMYAS1

HARLEQUIN "SILHOUETTE MAKES YOU A STAR!" CONTEST 1308
OFFICIAL RULES
NO PURCHASE NECESSARY TO ENTER

1. To enter, follow directions published in the offer to which you are responding. Contest begins June 1, 2001, and ends on September 28, 2001. Entries must be postmarked by September 28, 2001, and received by October 5, 2001. Enter by hand-printing (or typing) on an 8 ½" x 11" piece of paper your name, address (including zip code), contest number/name and attaching a script containing 500 words or less, along with drawings, photographs or magazine cutouts, or combinations thereof (i.e., collage) on no larger than 9" x 12" piece of paper, describing how the Silhouette books make romance come alive for you. Mail via first-class mail to: Harlequin "Silhouette Makes You a Star!" Contest 1308, (in the U.S.) P.O. Box 9069, Buffalo, NY 14269-9069, (in Canada) P.O. Box 637, Fort Erie, Ontario, Canada L2A 5X3. Limit one entry per person, household or organization.

2. Contests will be judged by a panel of members of the Harlequin editorial, marketing and public relations staff. Fifty percent of criteria will be judged against script and fifty percent will be judged against drawing, photographs and/or magazine cutouts. Judging criteria will be based on the following:

   - Sincerity—25%
   - Originality and Creativity—50%
   - Emotionally Compelling—25%

   In the event of a tie, duplicate prizes will be awarded. Decisions of the judges are final.

3. All entries become the property of Torstar Corp. and may be used for future promotional purposes. Entries will not be returned. No responsibility is assumed for lost, late, illegible, incomplete, inaccurate, nondelivered or misdirected mail.

4. Contest open only to residents of the U.S. (except Puerto Rico) and Canada who are 18 years of age or older, and is void wherever prohibited by law; all applicable laws and regulations apply. Any litigation within the Province of Quebec respecting the conduct or organization of a publicity contest may be submitted to the Régie des alcools, des courses et des jeux for a ruling. Any litigation respecting the awarding of a prize may be submitted to the Régie des alcools, des courses et des jeux only for the purpose of helping the parties reach a settlement. Employees and immediate family members of Torstar Corp. and D. L. Blair, Inc., their affiliates, subsidiaries and all other agencies, entities and persons connected with the use, marketing or conduct of this contest are not eligible to enter. Taxes on prizes are the sole responsibility of the winner. Acceptance of any prize offered constitutes permission to use winner's name, photograph or other likeness for the purposes of advertising, trade and promotion on behalf of Torstar Corp., its affiliates and subsidiaries without further compensation to the winner, unless prohibited by law.

5. Winner will be determined no later than November 30, 2001, and will be notified by mail. Winner will be required to sign and return an Affidavit of Eligibility/Release of Liability/Publicity Release form within 15 days after winner notification. Noncompliance within that time period may result in disqualification and an alternative winner may be selected. All travelers must execute a Release of Liability prior to ticketing and must possess required travel documents (e.g., passport, photo ID) where applicable. Trip must be booked by December 31, 2001, and completed within one year of notification. No substitution of prize permitted by winner. Torstar Corp. and D. L. Blair, Inc., their parents, affiliates and subsidiaries are not responsible for errors in printing of contest, entries and/or game pieces. In the event of printing or other errors that may result in unintended prize values or duplication of prizes, all affected game pieces or entries shall be null and void. **Purchase or acceptance of a product offer does not improve your chances of winning.**

6. Prizes: (1) Grand Prize—A 2-night/3-day trip for two (2) to New York City, including round-trip coach air transportation nearest winner's home and hotel accommodations (double occupancy) at The Plaza Hotel, a glamorous afternoon makeover at a trendy New York spa, $1,000 in U.S. spending money and an opportunity to have a professional photo taken and appear in a Silhouette advertisement (approximate retail value: $7,000). (10) Ten Runner-Up Prizes of gift packages (retail value $50 ea.). Prizes consist of only those items listed as part of the prize. Limit one prize per person. Prize is valued in U.S. currency.

7. For the name of the winner (available after December 31, 2001) send a self-addressed, stamped envelope to: Harlequin "Silhouette Makes You a Star!" Contest 1197 Winners, P.O. Box 4200 Blair, NE 68009-4200 or you may access the www.eHarlequin.com Web site through February 28, 2002.

Contest sponsored by Torstar Corp., P.O Box 9042, Buffalo, NY 14269-9042.

SRMYAS2

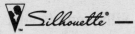 **Silhouette** —

where love comes alive—online...

eHARLEQUIN.com

your romantic
books

♥ Shop online! Visit Shop
eHarlequin and discover a
wide selection of new
releases and classic favorites
at great discounted prices.

♥ Read our daily and weekly
Internet exclusive serials, and
participate in our interactive
novel in the reading room.

♥ Ever dreamed of being a
writer? Enter your chapter
for a chance to become a
featured author in our
Writing Round Robin novel.

• • • • • •

your romantic
life

♥ Check out our feature articles
on dating, flirting and other
important romance topics
and get your daily love dose
with tips on how to keep the
romance alive every day.

• • • • • • •

your
community

♥ Have a Heart-to-Heart with
other members about the
latest books and meet your
favorite authors.

♥ Discuss your romantic
dilemma in the Tales from
the Heart message board.

your romantic
escapes

♥ Learn what the stars have
in store for you with our daily
Passionscopes and weekly
Erotiscopes.

♥ Get the latest scoop on
your favorite royals in
Royal Romance.

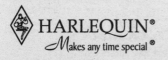